LOST IN THE MOUNTAINS

TONY MONTE

iUniverse LLC
Bloomington

LOST IN THE MOUNTAINS

iUniverse books may be ordered through booksellers or by contacting:

iUniverse LLC
1663 Liberty Drive
Bloomington, IN 47403
www.iuniverse.com
1-800-Authors (1-800-288-4677)

ISBN: 978-1-4917-3013-3 (sc)
ISBN: 978-1-4917-3012-6 (e)

Library of Congress Control Number: 2014906012

Printed in the United States of America.

iUniverse rev. date: 04/03/2014

2012

In Memory of

Eileen Monte my wife of 40 years

May 26, 1945—December 29,2002

Thanks to Mags Monte my second wife
for her help with this book.

"Some men are lucky to find one good
woman, few are lucky to find two"

Tony Monte

Chapter 1

THE JOURNEY BEGINS

1828

Shawn "Skip" Sullivan's father and mother were warned by the barking of the dogs, until arrows silenced them. Skip was hiding in the false floor of the cabin, where his mother and father had forced him to hide. From his hiding place, he could hear the sounds of his father fighting the Indians and his mother's screams of terror.

His father was a big man and he put up a brave fight, but there were too many of them, and soon he fell from a lance in his chest.

Shawn "Skip" Sullivan, stayed quiet long after the noise had stopped, but he was afraid to come out of hiding, for he did not know if the Indians had left or not, also he was afraid of what he might find.

Scared and trembling, he finally fell asleep. When he awoke, Skip knew it was early in the day. He was hungry and thirsty, there was no food in the hiding place, for the family never had enough to eat. Slowly he pushed on the trap door, it would not move, something heavy was lying across it.

Skip took after his father's side of the family. He was a big boy for his age, almost six feet tall, and one hundred and fifty pounds. He found an empty wooden box that had once been used to store potatoes. He took the box and put it below the door; he then stepped on to it and bent at the waist to get more leverage. Skip put his shoulder to the door and pushed with all his might. Whatever was on the door moved a little, he pushed harder, and soon had the door open. He looked all around and then came face to face with his dead father.

He started to cry when he saw his father's bloody head, the white hair was gone, and he looked around and saw his mother also scalped. Crying he looked around the cabin, there was not much of anything left, for the Indians had taken everything that was any good and destroyed the rest. There was some burlap bags scattered around the cabin, he took them and covered his mother and fathers heads, he could not stand to see them this way. He sat on the floor and cried for a long time, He did not know what he was going to do. The closest place for help he knew of was over thirty miles away, a trading post that he had been to once, and a long time ago. He did not even know what direction it was.

When the sun was high in the sky, he went outside to the creek for some water; he kneeled at the creek and drank heavily, then washed his dirty tear streaked face.

Skip knew he had to bury his mom and dad, so he walked over to the tool shed, the door was broken and hanging off its hinges. What the Indians did not take, they destroyed. Skip looked all around and found the shovel with a broken handle, thinking to himself, this will have to do.

His father was a big man and Skip knew he could not carry him far, so he dug the grave close to the front of the cabin. It took him most of the day to dig the grave, he decided to dig one wide grave and put them both in it together, laying side by side. Keeping the burlap over his father's face, so he did not have to look at him, He dragged him over to the grave and lowered him in the best he could; He did the same with his mom. Not wanting to throw dirt in his parents faces and not having anything to cover them with, he took the door that used to be on the tool shed and placed it gently over them, then he wearily filled in the grave, as the sun was just going down.

He looked through everything in the cabin, for things he could use and anything to eat. He found a knife that the Indians had missed, but no food. He went out back to the garden and found some potatoes, squash, and carrots. Thinking he would need some wood for a fire, he walked over to the stump where he always split the wood. The long handle axe was not there. He never put it into the stump, like his father always told him to do. Looking behind the stump, on the ground was the axe. He split some wood and carried it into the cabin. Laying the wood on the floor next to the turned over stove, he tipped the stove upright and put the stove pipe back the best he could, he found the flint on the floor and struck it against the axe and got a fire going. Finding a pot with a missing handle, he boiled the potatoes and carrots. When the food was cooked, Skip ate it all and drank the broth, and then he lay down near the remnants of the fire and fell into a deep exhausted sleep.

The next morning, Skip woke up at dawn. He was hungry and scared. He crawled up into the loft where he normally slept and looked all around, for anything he could use, the Indians ruined everything up there also, and he then remembered the box he had hidden under a loose board. Skip pulled up the loose board, his slingshot and his bag of round stones, were still there. He had practiced with the slingshot when his father could not see him, and was good with it. He thought, not much of a weapon, but he could kill small game with it. Skip put the bag and slingshot in his back pocket climbed down the ladder and went out of the cabin, He knew he could not stay here alone; somehow he had to find the trading post. Skip went to the grave and with tears running down his face, he said goodbye to his mom and dad.

He could not remember if the trading post was upstream or downstream, he choose upstream and started walking, with the axe over his shoulder and the knife in his belt, that and his slingshot in his back pocket was all that he had. After a few hours of walking he grew tired and hungry, he had nothing for breakfast and not much to eat last night. He reached in his back pocket and took out the slingshot and a round stone. Walking as quietly as he could, he searched the area, hoping to see a rabbit, squirrel, or any small game he could kill and eat. It was well past noon when he saw a rabbit, munching on some green weeds near the small stream. He was so hungry and was afraid he would miss, but he had to try. With shaking hands he pulled the slingshot as far back as it would go, he let go and saw the stone go plop in the water way over the rabbits head, luckily as the stone had hit the water quite a way from the rabbit it was not frightened and kept eating. Skip took out another stone, this time he took his time aiming, took a deep breath and let go, the rabbit jumped in the air and started flopping around on the ground, Skip picked up the axe, ran over and chopped off the rabbits head.

Skip knew enough to keep out of sight; he was still scared the Indians would come back. Down near the creek there was a lot of brush, He gathered some wood and headed for the brush, where he made a small fire, he cleaned the rabbit, put it on a stick, and cooked it, he ate every piece, and he even sucked the marrow out of the bones. It was still not enough, but it would have to do. The sun was going down, so he decided to sleep there. He put out the fire and covered the ashes with leaves so no one would see it, then covered himself with leaves and brush; he fell into a fitful sleep.

The next morning he left the brush and started walking upstream again. Not knowing he was headed the wrong way and going deeper into the mountains instead of towards the trading post.

He was much too scared and too young to notice the beauty of the approaching mountains. The cold clear water chilled by the snows higher up in the mountains running over the rocks, or the stillness of the beaver pond, broken only by the swimming of the beaver's and the jumping of the fish; but he would have to learn to notice everything if he wanted to stay alive.

Skip had been walking for three days now, living off rabbits, squirrels and anything he could kill or find. He thought he must have walked a hundred miles by now, but all he walked was thirty miles making ten miles a day. Late on the fourth day, Skip killed two partridges. He knew the sun would be going down soon, so he headed for the creek and looked for a place to camp. Near some brush and a large pine tree looked like a good place, as he approached the tree, he saw that someone had camped there before.

Close to the trees, Skip saw where an old fire had been and was partially covered with leaves, and a flattened area where someone had slept. That is when he really got scared, for he suddenly realized it was where he had camped the night before. He had spent the whole day walking in a big circle. Skip sank to the ground very scared, he pushed the leaves out of the old fire, gathered some small twigs, and made a new fire, he cleaned one of the birds, cooked it over the small fire, and ate every bit, and he looked hungrily at the second bird but decided he needed to save it for tomorrow. Then like all the nights before, he went to sleep still hungry.

Chapter 2

DULL KNIFE

The young Indian boy was mounted on a spotted pony, his bow with an arrow notched, was across his lap. The small doe he was tracking was not far away. Suddenly he felt his horse stagger, and he then heard the shot as his horse reared. He slid off the back of the pony, keeping hold of his bow, with the arrow still notched. The boy hit the ground landing on his back. His pony on wobbly legs stood a foot from him.

Looking under the pony's legs, he could see an Indian trying to reload his smooth bore rifle, drawing back his bow, as far as it would go, he let the arrow fly under the pony's stomach; the arrow flew true and hit the Indian in the chest.

The Indian looked down at his chest, not believing what had happened; he dropped his rifle and with both hands tried to pull the arrow out of his chest. With disbelief in his eyes he looked at the boy on the ground, and then fell over backwards, his body twitched a few times then he lay very still. The young boy was just getting up when his pony keeled over, landing on his leg pinning him to the ground.

He tried to pull his leg free, but the weight of his pony was too much. Knowing he would die if he did not free himself, he took out his knife and tried digging under the pony to free his trapped leg. After digging for hours, he was still no closer to getting his leg out from under his pony. He knew his only hope was to be found, but no one from the village would look for him for at least a few more days. Everyone knew he stayed out hunting for days at a time.

Hearing a noise beyond in the trees, he tried to reach his quiver with his arrows, but they had fallen out of reach. He knew if it was another hostile Indian, he was in big trouble. All he could do was wait with his knife ready. A knife is not much of a weapon when you are trapped under a horse on the ground.

Watching the trees where he heard the noise, he saw a young white boy come out of the trees; he could see the boy was afraid to approach him. He saw the boy only had a long axe for a weapon. It was not much of a weapon, but it was enough to kill him. He would show no fear, and would fight the best he could. With his knife at ready Dull Knife waited as the boy with the axe slowly approached him, he could see the boy was as scared as he was.

Chapter 3

Slim Toomey was a big man, weighing at least three hundred pounds. Many a man was fooled into thinking he was all-fat, but under that fat was a lot of hard muscle, for no one who was weak survived in the mountains.

Toomey had been watching Brownie and Big Jim for days now, waiting for them to split up. For no one worked together at the same location for long, he decided he would follow the one who moved further downstream to the next beaver dam.

The next morning Brownie saddled his horse and packed his mule, nodded to big Jim and headed down river, while Big Jim headed upstream. Toomey followed, and made camp about a mile further down and away from the beaver pond, where Brownie would trap. He settled down in his camp and did nothing but sit around, eat and sleep. He had enough supplies to last him a few weeks, he wanted to give Brownie enough time to trap a good amount of furs.

When his supplies were almost gone, he decided it was time. Toomey left his horse and mule in the makeshift corral. Carrying just his rifle, pistol, and possibles bag he headed for Brownies camp, he wanted to get there while Brownie would be out checking his traps. Upon reaching

Brownies camp, he looked around for a good place for an ambush. Carefully he chose a spot with two big pine trees and a lot of brush, to hide his big bulk. He found a good spot, Toomey then laid his rifle across a log aimed at the camp, and settled down to wait, knowing that Brownie would return just before dusk.

Toomey heard Brownie coming just before dark, looking through the brush, he could see Brownie carrying five beaver's at his side. Brownie stopped just before entering the camp and took a good look around, seeing or hearing nothing, he walked into the camp and dropped the beavers down next the dead campfire. He took out his flint and steel and soon had a small fire going; he cleaned, and skinned one beaver and cut up the meat for his evening meal. After putting the choice parts over a split to cook, he then began skinning and cleaning the rest of his catch. As lazy as Toomey was, he would wait for the skinning to be done. Toomey wanted the meat that was cooking, but being the coward he is, he decided to wait until Brownie was in his robes. Brownie skinned and staked out the skins to dry; he ate his meal, and turned in for the night. The fire was just coals, but still it cast enough light for Toomey to see Brownie with his back to him. Front or back made no difference to Toomey, with the hammer already pulled back on the rifle; he took aim and shot Brownie in the middle of the back where the heart would be.

Brownie never knew what hit him, he was dead instantly. Toomey walked over to Brownie, with a pistol in his hand, ready in case Brownie was not dead. With the pistol aimed at Brownies head, he put his foot under him and rolled him over, seeing the big hole in his chest where his heart was; he knew the trapper was dead. Toomey put some wood on the fire and cut up some of the beaver meat and put it on the split to cook, then he started getting all the plews and Brownies belongings together. There were a lot of plews; Brownie had worked hard while Toomey lazed around camp waiting. Toomey knew he could not take everything; he would to leave the rifle and pistols, but would take all the powder and balls.

After eating the meat, he walked over to Brownie, took out his knife, and scalped the trapper, wanting anyone who found Brownie to think that Indians killed him.

Toomey took Brownies horse and rode the mile in the dark to where he left, his own horse and pack mule. Without any delay, he led them back to the Brownies camp. By the time he got back, the meat was cooked; he ate every piece and without a thought for the dead trapper lying close by he turned in for the night.

At dawn, he packed all the plews and whatever he could take on the two mules, and headed for Horse Creek. Where the Rendezvous of 1835, would be held that year.

Big Jim had just got into his robes when he heard the shot, he knew it came from where Brownie was, He listened for any more shots, but there were none, one shot could mean almost anything, and more could have meant Indians or some kind of trouble. He knew he would have to check it out at first light. Jim tossed and turned all night, worrying about Brownie.

At first light, Jim saddled his horse and headed up river to Brownies camp, Jim was not prepared for what he found, upon reaching the camp, he saw Brownie still in his robes, he knew then that his friend, and partner was dead, you could never ride up on Brownie.

When Jim saw that Brownie had been scalped, he looked all around for sign, He knew it was done by one man, a white man, and by the size and depth of the tracks, he knew it was a large and heavy man.

He knew with certainty it was Toomey; with his green river knife and a pan he dug a grave as deep as he could, with much sadness he wrapped Brownie in his robe, lowered him into the grave, and filled it in.

Then and there, he promised Brownie, he would find Toomey and kill him.

He would leave him to rot and be eaten by the animals just as he had left his friend, if it was the last thing he ever did.

Chapter 4

When Skip awoke the next morning, he was cold, for the higher up he got the colder it got. Skip cleaned and plucked the feathers off the second partridge made a fire and ate the small bird. He put out the fire, gathered his meager possessions, and headed upstream. This time he was going to keep the creek in sight and to his left. For the next two weeks, Skip made better time, though cold and hungry, never enough catching enough rabbits or squirrels. Sometimes he got lucky and found some edible berries. He kept all the rabbit skins and used them for gloves and anything he could think of to keep warm.

The creek had split into two different streams, and he did not know what one to follow, he knew his only hope was to find someone or someplace. He learned to keep his eyes open, mostly to look for anything he could eat. He was heading for the creek looking for berries when he heard the shot, Skip knew it could be help or it could be an Indian and death. As quietly as he could he headed in the direction of the shot, hiding behind a big pine tree he saw a horse lying down, but the horse did not move, slowly he approached the horse. When he got close enough he saw an Indian lying under the horse.

After what had happened at the cabin, he was terrified. Skip hid behind a tree and watched for a long time, he could see that it was a young boy about his age, and the boy was pinned under the horse, digging frantically with his knife trying to free himself. Slowly he walked to the boy and the dead horse. The boy watched Skip as he approached him.

The young Indian boy had heard Skip coming a mile away, for he made more noise than a wounded bear. With his hand on his knife, he waited, when he saw it was a white boy he pointed the knife at Skip.

"I won't hurt you"; said Skip. The boy looked at Skip, waved his knife, and said something, but Skip had no idea what he was saying.

Skip laid down the knife and axe on the ground, and pointed to the knife in the Indians hand.

The Indian boy put his knife down also. Skip moved over to him and tried to lift the horse off the boy's leg. He could not budge the horse. Skip made the motion for digging, then picked up the boys knife and dug under the horse on both sides and under the boy's leg. After what seemed like hours he reached under the boy's arms and pulled him gently out from under the dead horse.

The boy's leg was not broken, but was very sore, after a short while, he could stand on it and walk around. Skip pointed at himself and said "Skip"; the boy repeated his name in very good English.

The boy knew English but did the same, pointing to his knife, "Me, Dull Knife".

Dull knife picked up his belongings, knife, bow and arrows, and blanket, and then walked over to the dead Indian. He took the rifle and powder horn and all the

Indian had, he then motioned for Skip to follow him. Skip picked up the few belongings he had and followed.

About an hour before sunset, they smelled smoke. Dull Knife pinched Skip's skin and pointed at a stand of trees.

Slowly they crept through the woods, trying not to make any noise; Skip could not have stepped on more twigs if he had tried. Dull Knife gave him a dirty look.

Skip had never been taught how to move without making noise, or how to live off the land. Hiding behind a large pine tree, they saw a white man sitting at a very small fire, smoking a pipe; and eating.

All Skip could look at was the food the old trapper was eating.

Chapter 5

The old mountain man was sitting at his fire. With his left leg in a splint, and across his lap was his rifle and homemade crutch. A week earlier while tending his traps, with the murder of Browne on his mind, Jim wanted to hurry after Toomey and that made him careless.

Jim had, had three prime beaver lying on the bank of the pond. He was getting his fourth, when he slipped at the edge of the pond and broke his leg.

The shock of the cold water kept him from passing out, the pain was great and to pass out was certain death. Living in the mountains for the last twenty or so years, made him as tough as any man could be, his skin was like old leather, brown and tough. He pulled his upper body and his right leg out of the water, leaving the broken leg in the cold water, the cold helped with the pain and helped to keep the swelling down. With his skinning knife, he cut his deerskin pants just up to the knee, for the break was below the knee in the shinbone. He knew he was lucky it was not the upper part of the leg. He skinned and cleaned the three beavers, keeping the meat to eat; knowing it was going to be hard to get game now. Grabbing a tree limb within his reach, the old man pulled himself from the water.

Looking around he saw the root of the tree he had tripped over, sliding over to the tree, using both hands he put his foot under the root, held his breath, then he pulled back as hard as he could, the pain was great, and if the leg were not numbed by the cold water he would have blacked out. He lay on his back until the pain eased up, then wrapped the beaver plews around his leg and then put splints on both sides of his leg, tying them top, and bottom with some rawhide strips he kept in his belt. He knew he had to get away from the pond and out of sight. Knowing it would be a few days before he could get back to his camp, which was a half mile away. He began dragging himself, his gun, and the beaver meat over to the spot, he chose for a makeshift camp. He could not look for Toomey until his leg was healed, but promised himself he would find Toomey, if it was the last thing he ever did.

For three days, he stayed at his temporary camp, dragging himself twice a day to soak his leg in the cold water to keep the swelling down. As the skins dried, they became tighter and made a good cast for his leg, the beaver meat was just about gone; it was time to make for his old camp. Taking his gun and using the crutch he had made, he headed for his camp; he hoped his mule was still there.

It took most of the day to reach his home camp, the sun was just starting to go down, his arm was sore from the crutch, but he knew he had to get a fire going and picket the mule on some new grass. Moving the mule was easy, he pulled the pin from the ground and with his arm around the mule's neck, Jim allowed the mule to walk to new grass. After putting the pin in the ground, the old mountain man hobbled to the fire pit. With steel and flint, he got a fire going and cooked some of the beaver meat, there would be one left for tomorrow. Talking aloud Jim said; "It will be hard to find that murdering bastard now Brownie, but find him I will."

Dull knife pointed to the old man, and in English whispered to Skip; "Leaves no tracks".

The old man looked over to where the two boys were crouched behind some brush; "Are you boys going to hide there all day? If you're friendly come on in." The boys got up and walked into the camp.

"Hello my name is Skip and this is Dull Knife."

"Come sit" said the old man.

"You are, Leave No Track's"; said Dull Knife.

"That's what you Indians call me; but I sure been leaving a lot of tracks with this crutch making holes in the ground, said the old man, White men call me Big Jim", for he was very big and tall. He cut off two pieces of meat and gave it to the boys, not much but it's all I got."

Skip ate his so fast he almost choked.

"A bit hungry are you boy?"

"Yes sir, I been living on rabbits and berries for a while now, and not much of either."

"Well unless you can hunt we all will starve."

"Me show", said Dull knife.

Big Jim; Looking at Skip asked; "Can you shoot?"

"No I never shot a gun before."

"Well I'm not giving my gun to an Indian, that's for sure."

"Me hunt with bow, Skip save Dull Knife life, me help, find deer in morning."

"You boys grab the extra robe over there." Big Jim covered himself with his robe and went to sleep, and the boys did the same.

When morning came, Dull Knife was gone. Skip looked around for him.

"He left before first light, either went hunting or left us, time will tell."

"Can I ask why you have two of everything Big Jim"?

"You are young, so I won't be mad at you, but you best learn, not to ask people their business. If they want you to know something about themselves, they will tell you."

"I had a partner, his name was Brownie." "We split up, he trapped the pond about a mile or two north of here, and I trapped this one."

"We would meet here every month or so. A few evenings ago I heard a shot, I knew it came from his camp, I was worried and headed to check it out." "When I was close to his camp, I knew something was not right, it was close to breakfast time, and I smelled no smoke. I approached very slow and stood behind a big tree, looking the camp over very good." "He saw Brownies feet under his robe, there was no fire, and if he was okay, he would be making breakfast and getting ready to go check out his lines. When I was sure no one was around I walked into the camp and called his name, No answer."

"I pulled the robe off him, he was lying on his back, and I could see he was dead, he had been shot, most likely in the back and scalped. There were no plews around; someone had killed him for the plews." "I looked all around the camp, his rifle and pistol was still there, he must have had a lot of plews, or the thief would have taken his gun and robe. His powder and balls were gone though, so was his horse and mule. So the killers must have taken all they could carry." "I studied the ground for tracks, all I could find were tracks of one man, and the tracks were very deep, the man had to be very heavy, that's how I knew it was Slim Toomey." "I had a fight with Toomey back in twenty-five, at the first Rendezvous, I wish I had killed him, and I would have if Brownie and Skeeter hadn't of pulled me off him, If I killed the fat pig, Brownie would still be alive."

"Well I buried my friend and brought what was left back to my camp, I promised Brownie I would find Toomey and kill him." "Well no one leaves his traps or beavers, so I went to get my traps and whatever beavers were in them, I was in a hurry to track Toomey and kill him, that made me careless and that's how I broke my leg and why I have two of everything." "If you stay with me boy I will teach you how to trap and live in the mountains."

"I have nowhere to go, and don't think I could live long alone out here, I will be happy to stay with you and help, Big Jim."

"I will call you Skip and you call me Jim."

"Yes Sir Jim."

"No sir, just Jim."

"Ok Jim."

Chapter 6

Later that day Dull Knife showed up with a small Doe. "I bring my friends meat, I must go back to my village, been gone too long, and people will look for me."

Skip walked over to Dull Knife and held out his hand, Dull Knife took his hand and said. "Skip, Friend". Skip shook his hand and said "Friend". Then Dull Knife left.

"This meat won't last forever, you have to learn to hunt, shoot, and set my traps."

"Bring that rifle and possible bag over here, first you need to learn how to load the rifle."

Skip replied; "I know how to load the rifle, my father showed me, but said he did not have enough powder and shot to teach me to shoot".

"Well we don't have enough for you to practice with either, I want you to get use to the rifle, practice aiming and squeezing the trigger. You will have to practice at live game, and do not shoot at anything small, just deer; if by chance you come across a bear of any kind just back away slowly and pray it do not come after you. If you see any Indians hide and stay quiet for a long time."

"Now bring me those traps and the small bag next to them." Big Jim then proceeded to teach him how to set traps.

That night Skip fell asleep with a full belly for the first time in over a month.

The next morning Jim showed Skip how to dry some of the meat into Jerky and make coffee and biscuits, with the little that was left.

"Ok boy, It's time for you to set the traps, just take three, I don't want you going too far and getting lost, do everything like I told you." Oh and by chance if a deer runs into you, shoot it; I don't see you sneaking up on one with the noise you make, and put this pistol in your belt."

Skip put the pistol in his belt, picked up the rifle, traps and possible bag and headed for the stream and the beaver pond. He did not want Big Jim to know how scared he was; he tried to be as quiet as he could, not because he wanted to shoot a deer, but because he was still afraid of Indians.

When he reached the pond, he looked for a place like the one Jim described to him. He found a limb that he could use for a stake.

He drove the stake into the ground with Jim's hatchet, and then took a trap to set; he hated the smell of the castrom. He had to set the trap three times before it stopped springing off; next, he put the loop over the stake. Then stepped into the cold water and set the trap, just deep enough so the beaver would drown, before it had a chance to chew off its leg. On his way to set the last trap, he kicked up a deer, but it was long gone by the time he got the rifle up to his shoulder.

Skip headed back to the camp, looking for something to shoot; he wanted to try the rifle in a bad way. He came upon a rabbit that was eating some wild cabbage or something like that; he did not know for sure what it was. Bringing the rifle up to his shoulder, ready to shoot, he remembered what Jim told him, he lowered the rifle and set it against a tree, then took out his slingshot, put in a round stone, pulled back and let go. Thinking, looks like rabbit again, and if the rabbit could eat that green stuff so could they.

He cleaned the rabbit, and picked some of the cabbage type stuff and headed for camp.

As he got close to the camp, he tried to sneak up on Jim.

"Better then the first time boy. Instead of sounding like a bull buffalo, you sound more like a buffalo cow." Har, har.

Skip smiled, "Someday I will sneak up on you".

"I hope so boy, or you won't live long."

"It's easy for you and Dull Knife, I was never showed how to move in the woods; I got a rabbit and some green stuff to eat."

"Did you hide the guts?"

"No why would I do that?"

"Well boy, some Indian comes along he will know we are around, but then again I am sure you left enough tracks a blind man could follow."

Jim knew he was being hard on the boy, but if the boy was going to survive in the mountains, he had to learn, or die.

"Well Jim, I set the traps and got us something to eat, I will learn."

"I think you will boy, if you live long enough; there are things you have to understand out here.

"An Indian will kill you just because you are white. A white man will kill you just as fast for anything you have. Most Indians are honorable, that young boy you helped will be your friend for life. Always remember this, the

Blackfeet will never be your friend, they will kill you just because you are white, they hate all white men".

"Once this leg heals I will be able to show you how to do things."

Skip cut the rabbit into chunks and made a stew with the green stuff and what was left of Jims supplies.

After they were done, eating Jim told him they had to get something bigger than a rabbit.

"Skip; tomorrow you have to go out and check the traps. Then look around near the pond for deer tracks, and then sit there as quiet as you can, without moving. If you are still, a deer cannot tell what you are, movement, smell and noise is what spooks them. Now let's eat that stew and turn in for the night."

Chapter 7

The first rays of sun were just starting to come over the top of the trees, when Skip woke up. Jim already had a fire going. "You sure like to sleep boy."

"I can't do much in the dark, Big Jim."

"No I guess you can't boy; are you going to get us some good meat today?"

"After I check the traps, I will sit there all day if I have to."

"Now you're sounding like a hunter, do you know what chicory looks like?"

"Yep that's all we drank at home, we could not afford coffee." Skip got a little teary eyed as he thought of home.

"I know you miss your home and parents Skip. The mountains are a beautiful place, but they are a very dangerous place, you have to stay alert at all times, you got to look for signs to see if anyone has been around, use your eyes and hearing, even use your nose."

"I may seem hard on you boy, but I want to keep you alive, for both our sakes."

"I understand Big Jim, tonight we will eat venison."

"Listen to me boy, after you shoot that rifle, before you move a foot, you reload, and if you should drop a deer, you sit still for five or ten minutes and look all around, you never know if any Indians are around, and if you have to shoot at someone you shoot to kill or they will kill you."

"Ok Jim, see you later."

"I sure do hope so boy."

With his hatchet and knife in his belt, shot pouch and powder horn over his shoulder, Skip picked up the rifle and started to leave.

"Take this pistols too boy."

Skip took the pistol from Jim and put it in his belt then headed for the pond.

Doing as Jim told him, he took a different way to the pond, not wanting to make a trail to the camp, he would come back a different way. Every twenty feet or so he would stop, look and listen, and check his back trail, it took longer this way, but he would do as Jim told him.

Upon reaching the first trap, he was disappointed to see nothing was in it, but the trap was still set, so he just moved on. The next two had a beaver in them; he took both beavers from the traps then reset them both. Skip then looked around for deer tracks, about a hundred yards from the last trap, he found deer sign. And not being an experienced hunter, he had no idea if the tracks were hours, days, or months old, but any tracks were better than none at all. Looking around he saw a large log down near a pine tree. With his back against the tree and his rifle resting on the log, he waited with the wind in his face.

For the first time he looked all around and saw why Big Jim loved the mountains. The pond was like a big sheet of glass; the only movement was where the stream emptied into the pond causing ripples and waves, Skip noticed the lush grass in the meadow, the wild flowers and the blue sky, and the clean fresh mountain air. Skip was already starting to love the mountains and knew if he survived, they would always be his home.

To Skip it seemed like he waited hours and saw nothing, then he heard some noise off to his right, He thought a deer, or maybe an Indian, that got him scared, he lowered himself closer to the ground, just peeking over the log, there at the pond was a nice fat doe getting a drink.

Slowly he swung the rifle around and pulled back the hammer, it came back with a click; the doe pulled its head up fast and looked all around. Skip froze, after checking that all was safe the doe began to drink. Skip's heart was beating so fast and loud, he was sure the deer would hear it. With his hands shaking, he aimed just behind the doe's left leg, as Jim had told him to do, taking in a deep breath, he slowly squeezed the trigger, the rifle boomed and kicked back against his shoulder. The doe jumped straight up in the air, then fell down kicking. He started to get up and run to the deer. But then he heard Jim's words, reload before even taking a step, then sit for five or ten minutes, and look all around and listen. Taking the powered horn from around his neck, and pouring the right amount of powder in his hand, and then poured the powder down the barrel, then taking a patch and ball he rammed the ball home, and then inserted a cap on the nipple. Sitting there with his heart beating and his hands shaking with excitement and fear he waited. He looked all around and listened for any noise, and then he slowly got up and walked over to the deer.

The doe was not dead and looked at him with big fearful eyes, Skip felt bad killing the animal, but he knew it was his life or hers. They needed the meat. Pulling out his knife he knelt and slit the doe's throat, then took a good look all around, he was still afraid that some Indian might be close, and had heard the shot. He cleaned the deer and buried the guts as Jim told him to do. Thinking to himself, I do not know why I have to bury the insides; some animal will dig it up any ways. It was a small doe and was no problem to carry it over his shoulder, one more look around and Skip headed back for camp.

Chapter 8

THE CAT

It had been a hard and long winter in the mountains, game was scarce and the Mountain Lion was starving, The heard the shot and knew what it was for she had been slightly wounded by a human before, just a slight crease along her back, she should have been afraid, but the hunger took away her fear. Slowly the big skinny cat limped towards the noise and soon picked up the scent of blood, the pain in her left paw was so bad she could never touch the ground with it.

It was over a month now that she had her first and last encounter with the porcupine, she had sneaked up on the animal, it did not move, but she knew it was alive and she could eat it, with her left paw she swatted it with great force, flinging it through the air. She felt great pain in her paw and let out a ferocious scream. Angrily she bit down hard on the porcupine; all she got was more pain and more quills in her body. She retreated and tried to remove the quills with her teeth, she got most out, but two quills were deep in her front paw, and she had to leave them. By now, the paw was infected and she was crazy with pain and hunger. As she got closer to the doe, the smell of blood was driving her crazy. The big Cat did not notice the man or did not care. All she could see and smell was the deer, when the cat was close enough she sprung onto the back of the doe, knocking the man down, all she could think of was the meat and tore a hunk out of the deer and swallowed it, then tore out another chunk

Skip rolled over a few feet away from the big cat, pulled out the pistol, and pulled back the hammer and shot the cat in the head. The cat died instantly.

Shaking, Skip got to his feet, again he heard Jims voice, always reload your guns, he did so, then picked up the deer and headed back for camp. He learned another lesson that day; do not just look in front, but to look to the sides and your back trail also.

As he walked into the camp, he saw Jim shake his head, "Two shots for one deer is not good."

"One shot for the deer and one for the cat that jumped me."

"You had an encounter with a mountain lion and survived?"

"The cat was skin and bones and wounded, it had a bad paw, it didn't even pay any attention to me; all the lion wanted was the deer."

"Well I'm glad of that, lets skin her and eat; I'm starving."

Skip skinned the deer; he cut off two big chunks and tossed them to Jim to cook. Jim put two big steaks over the split and watched, as the meat sizzled and cooked, neither had a good meal in over a weak, when the meat was half cooked, Jim tossed one of the steaks to Skip.

As they sat around the campfire, Big Jim told Skip how he came to the mountains and became a trapper. Skip sat quietly and listened to Big Jim's life story.

The year was about 1810 when I came west to the Shinning Mountains. I was around eighteen when I left Albany, New York. I was young and strong and feared no man, while sitting in a saloon drinking a beer, a loud mouth was telling everyone how tough he was, he bumped into my arm and knocked the beer from my hand spilling the beer all over me and him. Well he started hollering at me like it was my fault.

I told him he was the one who caused it and he should buy me a beer, he said that will be a cold day in hell and he should beat the hell out of me for getting beer all over him.

I told him, now that would be a cold day in hell, and then I got up from my stool and faced him. well he took a big swing at me, I just ducked and came up with a right that hit him on the chin Well he fell backwards and hit his head on the bar, and slid down to the floor out cold, so I thought.

The bouncer walked on over to the man, and was starting to drag the loud mouth out of the bar. When he noticed the man was not breathing. He said the man was dead, I guess when he hit his head on the bar he cracked his skull. He said he was going to get the constable.

Well I got scared and left the bar in a hurry. I then went to see a friend of mine who just happened to be a lawyer, he told me I was in big trouble, and maybe I should disappear. I went home and got my belongings and what money I had, and headed west.

The fur trade was just getting started, so I looked around and asked a few questions, I was in a saloon and saw four trappers sitting and drinking beer, I went over to them and said I wanted to trap beaver. They looked me over and began to roar with laughter, I got mad and asked what was so funny, they laughed all the louder. One kicked a chair out and told me to have a seat, my temper was up, but I sat down anyways.

The one who told me to sit was about my age, he reached out his hand and said his name was Kit Carson, at the time that meant nothing to me; I shook his hand and said I am Jim.

He said you're a big one Jim, then he called me Big Jim, and that's how I got my name, I never told anyone my last name to this day.

Well Big Jim, Carson said, you are a green horn that is for sure, if you go into those mountains alone, you will never come out. I told him I did not plan to go alone, and was hoping I could partner up with one of you, and you would teach me.

Kit Carson asked why anyone should take me along and teach me how to trap and live in the mountains, I told him I would work hard and do what they told me to do.

Well they took me along and taught me all I know today; little did I know that Kit Carson was the king of trappers at that time. The others were well known mountain men also.

"So now you know why and how I came to the mountains, and you are the only one who knows why, I would like you to keep it that way".

I will never speak of it Jim, It is late so I am going to turn in, I am sure you will have plenty for me to do come daylight".

Skip rolled up in his robe and went to sleep. Big Jim thought to himself, the boy is learning, he might make a mountain man out of him yet.

Chapter 9

It was about a half hour before the sun rose, when Big Jim heard a slight noise that woke him. He listened and looked all around, he could hear nothing, but he could smell them, he had been around Indians all his life and he knew the smell.

Jim reached inside his buffalo robe and took out his pistol, cocked it and laid it on top of his robe, then did the same with his rifle. Lying along side of him was his crutch, slowly he picked it up, and then he reached out and poked Skip with it several times until Skip finally woke up. Skip looked over at Jim, there was just enough coals in the fire to cast enough light on Jim, Skip could see Jims finger over his mouth, signaling him to be quiet. Jim pointed to his guns sitting on top of his robe. Skip got the message, with shaking hands he reached under his robe and got his pistol, then got his rifle that was by his side.

Jim pointed to his eyes and then pointed behind him. Skip turned enough so he could see behind him. All the fears that he had back at the cabin, came back to him. With his heart pounding and his hands shaking, he picked up the pistol cocked it, and waited. As the sun came up, they came screaming, two from the front and two from the back Jim shot the first one with his rifle then the other with his pistol. Skip was so scared he froze.

"Shoot them." Screamed Jim

Like in a dream in slow motion, Skip raised his pistol and shot the one closest to him, then reached for his rifle, but he knew he was going to be too late, for the Indian was standing over the top of him, with a tomahawk. Skip knew it was all over for him; he closed his eyes and waited for the blow. Just as the tomahawk was coming down, an arrow entered the Indians chest; the Indian dropped the tomahawk and grabbed the arrow with both hands, trying to pull it out, when another one entered his heart, the Indian fell over backwards and moved no more.

Skip opened his eyes and there stood Dull Knife.

"Blackfeet, bad, hate all white men."

"Skip smiled and with a shaky voice said;" Thank you my friend".

"Stop yapping and load that rifle." Jim hollered; as he loaded his guns. "Then go see if you can find their horses, we can't stay here any longer."

"There are no horses, they come on foot, I saw them come your way so I followed."

Jim shook his head; "Dam just our bad luck, well I will have to ride the mule, we will have to hide the plews and come back for them when my leg is better."

"Jim, will there be time for me to get the traps and any beaver that are in them?"

"Yes it will take some time before they are missed, but don't take too long, with this leg we will be traveling slowly."

Skip grabbed his guns, shot pouch and powder and headed for the pond.

"I will help you": said Dull Knife.

Jim watched as the two boys hurried away, hoping they would not take all day.

With Dull Knife leading, the two boys headed for the beaver pond.

They hid behind some brush and looked the pond and surrounding area over, not seeing anyone they continued on; the first trap still had nothing in it, so Skip sprung it, put it over his shoulder and headed for the remaining two traps, each one had a beaver in them, they skinned the beavers and kept the meat. Skip put the traps over his shoulder and they headed back to the camp.

Upon reaching the camp, they saw Jim hobbling around getting things packed.

"Well hurry up and help me, I want to make tracks".

Dull knife shook his head: "He, who leaves no tracks, wants to leave tracks now."

Skip smiled; "He means he wants to leave here fast."

The boys helped pack all they could and buried what they could not take.

"You come to my village, be safe there".

"Do you think your people will welcome us there?" asked Jim.

"When I tell how Skip saves me, they will be friendly to you."

With Big Jim hanging on to the mules neck, he said "Lead on Dull Knife, and make sure you tell them, my mule is not for eating."

Chapter 10

They arrived at the Shoshone village ten days later; because of Jim's bad leg, they only made about five miles a day.

When Skip saw the village and all the Indians he became scared, the memories of the slaughter back at the cabin came to him again.

Dull Knife sensed Skips fear, "Do not be afraid of my people, the Shoshone have always been friends to the white man, come meet my family."

Dull Knife lifted the flap to the teepee and told Jim and Skip to enter.

Sitting around the fire was an old man, the old man motioned for Skip to sit on his left and for Jim to sit next to Skip.

"Looks like you got the place of honor Skip."

Skip said nothing and sat down, still a little afraid of being around so many Indians.

The old man took his pipe, and filled it with tobacco, he reached over to the fire and took out a small branch and lit the pipe. He blew smoke to the four corners of the earth, and then handed it to Skip.

Skip puffed on the pipe and coughed, then did as the old man did and passed the pipe to Jim, who did the same, Jim passed it to Dull Knife who did the same, then passed it back to Black Hawk, his father.

The old man took the pipe and said something in Shoshone.

Dull knife translated: "My father said, who helps my son helps me, and who is my sons friend is my friend; you can stay with us as long as you like, in the morning he will have a gift for the young man".

Dull Knifes mother gave them food, after they had eaten; Dull Knife rose and told them to follow him. Skip and Jim rose and followed Dull Knife, over to a nearby teepee, "This will be your home for as long as you want to stay".

Skip and Jim entered the teepee, there was a fire burning in the middle of the floor, and buffalo robes laid out for them, which was welcome for the night was chilly. They were both tired, so they fell asleep as soon as they got into the robes.

The next morning a young girl brought them food, she was about Skip's age, she had long brown braided hair and blue eyes, and she wore a soft doeskin dress that showed her slim body. Skip could not take his eyes off of her, for she was very pretty and Skip had not seen very many girls. "When you are through with eating, my father has a gift for you."

Skip was surprised and happy that she could speak English, for now he could talk to her. "My name is Skip, can you tell me yours?"

"I am Chimalis, in your language I am called, Blue Bird Eye, but they call me Yahto, it means Blue."

"I will call you Yahto, if that is ok?"

"That will be good Skip" Yahto smiled and left the teepee. Skip followed her with his eyes as she walked to leave the teepee, just before she ducked under the door flap she looked back over her shoulder and saw Skip looking at her, she gave him a shy smile and left.

Skip gobbled his food and headed for the opening in the teepee.

Big Jim laughed, "I think someone has fallen for a little Blue Bird".

When he stepped out of the teepee, there was Dull Knife, Holding a beautiful red roan horse. Skip looked all around for Yahto, but she was not around.

"Do you not like the horse Skip?"

"The horse is for me?"

"Yes a gift from my father."

"Wow I love him."

"That is good, but it is a mare."

"Okay I love her."

"Do you mean the horse or my sister?"

Skip got all red in the face, "I love the horse".

Dull Knife smiled, "I think you like Yahto too".

Skip walked over and rubbed the horses head.

Dull knife laughed, and handed Skip a bow and some arrows. "Leave horse, we go hunting."

Skip laughed, "That's a good name for my horse".

Dull Knife looked at Skip with a funny look, "What name is good for horse"?

Skip laughed, "Horse; that is what I will call her".

Dull Knife shook his head and mumbled, Horse, white men crazy sometimes.

Chapter 11

The two boys headed off towards the river, with Dull Knife in front; as usual, Skip was making so much noise he would scare a grizzle away.

Dull Knife turned with a little disgust on his face, "The first thing I must teach you is how to be quiet."

"What is the second thing?"

"You must learn patience; sometimes you may have to sit all day, before you see a deer."

"That's easy for you Dull Knife, you have been shown how to do that all your life, my father was a farmer and never taught me how to hunt or move in the woods."

"I know this Skip, and I will teach you these things, but it will take time. Today we will just walk in the woods and you will learn the way my father taught me."

As they entered the woods and stood still, Dull Knife said; listen, what you hear?

Skip listened for sounds, "I hear birds singing, and moving in the trees, when we came into the woods I heard something big, run away from us".

"That is good, always listen for these things, when all is quiet, it means something is scaring the animals, always listen for something that is not right. When you wake at night, there is no moon or stars, it is black out, you have to go to the bushes, how do you find your way?"

"I walk very careful so I don't trip and I feel with my hands, so I don't walk into anything."

"That is how you should always walk in the forest, like it is dark. Feel with your feet, if you feel anything do not put your foot down. Put it where there are no branches, walk slow, stop, and listen all the time, after a while you will do it without thinking."

As they walked through the forest, Skip tried to be quiet, but with his worn out boots, he could not feel the small twigs under his feet.

"When we get back, I will ask my sister to make you some moccasins."

Skip smiled at the mention of Chimalis.

"It is good you are trying, when you have moccasins on you will do better, now we will sit and watch for Deer."

After what seem like hours, Dull Knife touched Skip with his bow, and pointed off to one side, there was the largest buck Skip ever saw. Dull Knife indicated for Skip to shoot, he nodded and put an arrow in the bow, pulled it all the way back and let go, the arrow landed far away from the deer, the beast took off running. Dull Knife laughed quietly as he let go with his arrow, it buried deep just behind the buck's right shoulder, but the deer kept running.

"We will sit here for a while then go get the buck".

"But it ran away" said Skip.

"It will lie down and stiffen up, we will follow the blood trail, and the buck will be there". After about thirty minutes, Dull Knife rose and started walking, Skip followed. After walking about two hundred yards they found the buck, it was dead.

They skinned the buck, butchered it, and wrapped it in the hide.

"My sister will cure the hide and make something for you with it".

Then they headed back to the camp. As they approached the camp, a young buck was waiting for them. When they spotted the young man, Dull Knife warned Skip there would be trouble with that one.

"What did I do to him?" asked Skip.

"His name is Bold One, He likes Yahto, and all can tell you have eyes for her."

"Well I'm not going to fight with him."

As Skip went to walk around Bold One, he stuck out his foot and tripped Skip. Skip jumped up yelled angrily. "I will not fight with you"; and turned to leave. Bold One grabbed Skip by the shoulder and spun him around, "Like all white eyes, you are a coward"; in one swift movement, he pulled out his knife.

Swiftly, Dull Knife moved in front of Bold One, and knocked the knife to the ground "You know you cannot kill a guest in the village."

"He should leave here, Yahto is not for him, she is for me."

"That is not for you to decide, my father will have the say on who Yahto will make the Blanket walk with. I cannot fight for Skip, but I say there will be no weapons."

Ignoring Dull knife, Bold One charged Skip and drove him to the ground, Skip had never been in a fight before, and did not know what to do. He just wrapped his arms around Bold One and squeezed with all his strength, working on the farm and the last month surviving in the mountains, had built up Skips muscles. He was a lot stronger than most boys his age. Bold One let out a loud scream. You could hear his ribs crack.

Dull Knife pulled on Skips arms, "Let him go Skip, he is done".

Skip got up and looked down at Bold One who was in obvious pain on the ground.

"I am sorry I hurt him Dull knife, we should help him".

"No he would have killed you if he could have; he broke the village rules by attacking a guest. My father will deal with him later".

They walked off and left Bold One on the ground. When they reached the tepee, Skip told Big Jim what had happened, "Well I guess he should not have messed with you". said Jim, If you live long enough you are going to be a big man, most likely bigger than me".

"Now let's eat and get some sleep, they will be moving the village in a few days".

"How do you know that"? Skip asked.

"I can tell by the smell of the village, and soon winter will be on its way, so they will head for their winter camp". "Are you afraid you will not see your little Blue Eyes?"

"I just like to know what we are going to do".

"I plan on moving with the village, and when the beaver get their winter fur, I will trap. You can come with me if you like".

"Of course I am coming with you, we have to get Toomey don't we?"

"Yes, we will find him at the next Rendezvous, now let's hit the robes".

Chapter 12

Toomey headed for the 1833 Rendezvous at Horse Creek.

He knew of a Ute's village along the way, where he could trade Brownies horse and mule, showing up at the Rendezvous with Brownies mounts would not be wise.

When he reached the village, he looked for his friend Flying Eagle, finding him he swapped the mule and horse, for two scrawny ponies. He knew he had got the bad end of the deal but all he wanted them for was to get the furs to the rendezvous. When he got the hides there, he would have no more use for the ponies and he would trade them for anything he could get.

Upon reaching the rendezvous, he looked around to see who was buying. He finally came on Bents table, Bent was known by all, as a man who would not cheat you, and always gave a fair price. Leaving his furs to be graded he walked around looking for a place to get free food.

At one camp he saw six men sitting around the fire eating, Toomey walked over and greeted the group, too late he noticed Skeeter.

"Have a seat Toomey, meats done".

"Thanks Skeeter, I am a bit hungry".

Everyone laughed, when Donavan said, "When aren't you hungry?"

Toomey sat down, took out his knife and cut some meat off the haunch that was on the split, He noticed that Skeeter was staring at him.

"Something on your mind: Skeeter?"

"I just noticed you had a lot of fine plews this year, Toomey."

"Yea I had a good year."

"You must have trapped a lot of ponds, to get that many plews, I was wondering if you ran across Big Jim and Brownie."

"can't say that I did."

"Then why do you have Brownies powder horn?"

"Did this one belong to Brownie? I traded some Indian for it."

Well Brownie and Big Jim have not showed up yet, and if they're not here by tomorrow, I'm going looking for them, and I better find them okay."

"What are you getting at Skeeter?"

"Just funny you have about four times as many plews then you ever had, and for the first time in as long as I can remember Brownie is late to the Rendezvous. I would say, add to all that, you show up with Brownies powder horn. Jest saying"

"A man could get killed talking like that Skeeter."

"You're welcome to try, and if I find any harm came to either of them, There will be more than talking done about it. Don't fer a minute think this is the end of this conversation, we will talk more about this".

Toomey got up and walked away.

"If he did either of them in, I will skin that fat bastard alive."

"When you leaving Skeeter?" asked Crown.

"I'm leaving at first light."

"You want company?"

"Sure Crown, I would love to have you along."

"Thanks, it's always better to have someone with you, to watch your back. These days you never can tell who you might meet up with".

Chapter 13

Skip rose before the sun was up and started a fire to cook some meat.

There was a scratching at the flap of the teepee; Skip had learned this was the Indian way of knocking.

"Come in". Skip said.

Yahto, entered the teepee, she was holding two pair of moccasins, one low cut, and one high.

She held the moccasins out in front of her. "I make for you, Skip".

Skip rose and walked over to her and took the moccasins, "Thank you, Yahto".

"Yahto, we will move with the village, and then find our own place to trap beaver, can I come back and see you, when there is time".

"I would like that Skip, I must go back now".

Skip watched her walk away, with a longing he never felt before.

Jim was smiling as he pretended to be sleeping, thinking that Skip was smitten badly.

Giving a loud yawn and sitting up, "Were you talking to someone?" Jim asked.

"Yes, Yahto made me moccasins".

"Jim, what are we going to do for powder?"

"I been thinking on that", we might have to go back for the plews we buried and head for a trading post, before we start trapping again, the fur will not be good enough to trap for another month, that will give us enough time".

"We will be coming back to the tribe wont we?"

"For a while, but we have to find our own place to live and trap".

There was a lot of noise in the camp, dogs barking, and men hooting.

Skip grabbed his rifle went out the teepee and headed for the end of the village where the noise was coming from, there he saw Dull Knife.

"What is all the yelling are we being attacked?"

"No two white men are in the village."

Seeing the white men Skip walked over to them, they were, mountain men dressed the same him and Big Jim. They wore buckskin and each had a Hawken rifle and two pistols, a large knife in their belts, each man was leading a pack mule.

As Skip was looking them over, they were doing the same to him. "Hello my name is Skip Sullivan."

The bigger of the two said; "First thing I want to know, green horn, is where you got that rifle?"

Big Jim stepped to the front, "From me Skeeter".

Skeeter jumped down and the two men hugged each other.

"Where is Brownie, Jim?"

"It saddens me to say Skeeter, he was put under."

You could see the sadness in Skeeter's eyes. "Blackfeet he asked?"

"No that murdering bastard Toomey shot him in his robes then scalped him, to make it look like Indians done it, and stole all his plews, when I find him, I'm going to kill him slow and leave him for the wolves to eat."

"Toomey was at the Rendezvous; I thought he had a lot of plews, more than he ever trapped in two years, when you and Brownie did not show, I came looking."

"Who's your partner?"

"Don't know his real name, he's from England, so we just call him Crown".

"Howdy Crown, That young girl you're looking at, sort of belongs to Skip, I would leave her be if I was you. Come we will eat".

As they walked to Jim and Skip's teepee, "I don't think I will fear that green horn". Crown said.

Skeeter turned back towards Crown, "Maybe not, He's a big boy for his age, but you better fear Big Jim".

When they entered the teepee Jim told them to help themselves to the meat cooking on the split over the red-hot coals that would flare up when the grease from the meat fell on them.

Jim explained how he broke his leg and could not trail Toomey.

"What are your plans Jim"? Skeeter asked.

"Well the village is going to move to a valley just below the mountains, Skip and me will go up higher to a nice valley with a nice stream in it, I want to see what there is for beaver up there, Do you have some shot and extra powder, I can trade some plews for.

"I have enough to get you through the winter. What about Toomey?"

"I'm hoping to catch up with him at the next Rendezvous".

"Well Jim, we brought some things to trade, so we are going to set up, then leave at dawn".

Skeeter and Crown left the teepee and set blankets on the ground with their trade goods.

Skip started to follow the two traders.

"Skip, half of the plews are yours, if you see anything you want trade for it".

Skip looked at the goods lying on the blanket; he chose a Green river knife and a small hatchet. Then he saw some red and orange ribbons, assortment of beads and some sewing needles, he placed them in a pile and asked Skeeter how much?

"Two pelts should cover it".

Skip left then came back with two pelts and handed them to Skeeter, picked up his goods and left. As he headed for Yahto's teepee, he heard a dog cry out, he saw a big Indian hitting the dog with a club. He hurried over to the Indian and grabbed the club.

Not far away, Dull Knife saw what was going on, he knew there would be trouble, so he hurried over and grabbed Skips arm.

Dull Knife told Skip, "It is his dog he can do what he wants with it".

Dull Knife turned to the big Indian, "Sorry for my friend's behavior Tall Oak, He does not know our ways".

Tall Oak nodded.

"Dull Knife; ask him if he will trade for the dog, I will give him my long axe".

Dull Knife did as Skip asked; Tall Oak smiled and nodded.

Skip went back to the teepee, got the axe, and handed it to Tall Oak.

Tall Oak grabbed the axe and smiled. "Good trade for Tall Oak, bad for white man", he laughed and walked away.

Dull Knife told Skip that he gave too much for the dog.

Skip shrugged his shoulders then tied a piece of red ribbon around the dog's neck, with the dog on the raw hide leash, he then walked out to where his big red roan horse was picketed and tied a piece of red ribbon in the horses mane, now all would know they belonged to him. He walked back to the teepee and tied the dog to a stake in the ground, got some meat out of the teepee and gave it to the big black, starving skinny dog.

With the goods he traded for in his hands, he walked over to Yahto's teepee, she was outside working on a buffalo robe, she rose when he came to her, He handed her the beads, ribbon, and sewing awl, and with a big smile, she thanked him.

Still being very shy, he smiled and walked back to his teepee, went inside and grabbed his Hawken and pistols, stuck them in his belt with his new hatchet and Green River Knife, and headed for his horse, the big black skinny dog started whining.

Skip walked back to the dog. "You want to come dog".

He bent down and untied the whining animal, "come on dog", the boy and his new dog headed for his horse.

Bold one had watched Skip take this ride before, knowing the way he would go, leaving his bow and arrows behind, he left the village at a fast trot ignoring his cracked ribs, Foolish white men always take the same trail, he headed for the place where he would kill him, Yahto was to be his and his alone.

When he reached the big oak tree he climbed up to the large limb and waited, He knew he could have put an arrow in him, but he wanted the white man to know who killed him. He did not have long to wait, When Skip was under him, knife in hand he leaped from the tree

A slow ride through the forest with dog following, he was no longer afraid, for he had learned much from Dull knife and Big Jim.

Skip took in the beauty of the forest. The tall trees, birds singing, and squirrels' were jumping from tree to tree, and high above him a majestic Eagle soared. He was happy, for Yahto gave him a big, pretty smile. But by being happy, he also got careless and stopped paying attention to things around him. Skip never noticed that the birds had stopped singing and the squirrels stopped, playing, He had Yahto on his mind.

Dog gave a deep growl and snapped Skip from his daydreaming just as a shadow fell across him. He tried to bring his rifle around, but was too late; the Indian was upon him, with a long knife in his hand. Skips rifle fell from his hand as he was falling; swiftly he pulled his knife from his belt. The two hit the ground hard with the Indian on top. Skip was stunned, winded for a moment, and could not move, just as the knife came down, a black streak hit the Indian and knocked him off Skip. Bold One flung the big skinny dog off him and turned back towards Skip. The dog had given Skip enough time to come around; he drew his pistol and shot the Indian as he was diving at him. The Indian gave a grunt, fell on his face, and laid still.

Skip grabbed his rifle and took a good look around, not seeing or hearing anything he reloaded his pistol, then walked over and patted dog, with a soft voice he said good boy. Dog whined and wagged his tail. A great friendship had started.

Skip walked over turned the dead Indian over. Much to his surprise, it was Bold One. This would be the last time he would try to hurt Skip.

Skip gave a low whistle and the red roan came as he had trained him to do. He picked up Bold One and put him across the horse's back, at the smell of blood, the horse became skittish, Skip talked softly, and gently stroked the frightened horse's head and neck, he soon had the big animal settled down. With the reins in hand and Dog at his heels, he headed back to the village. What he had planned to be a nice quiet ride in the forest was ruined. Skip was learning that there is never a safe or quiet time in the wilderness; one has to always be on guard, if he wants to survive in the mountains

As he entered the village, he was worried what would happen, a white man had killed one of their own. Dull knife saw Skip come in to the village and called his father from the teepee, they stood waiting as Skip came to them.

"I am sad to bring Bold One in like this, he jumped me in the forest, I had no choice but to shoot him. I did not know who he was till after I shot him. He wanted to kill me".

The entire village was gathered around to see what Chief Black Hawk would do. The Chief looked around and said to his people.

"Bold One has broken the rules again and attacked a guest in our village, if he had killed my son's friend, He would have banished him from the tribe. There will be no more talk of this". Then turned and entered his teepee. Dull Knife took the red Roans reins; "I will take Bold One to his father". Skip went to his teepee to explain what had happened to Big Jim.

Chapter 14

The next morning the tribe began to move the village closer to the big valley, at the base of the mountain.

Skip was amazed at how everyone worked together, without anyone being in charge. The woman took down the teepees and stacked all their things on the travois, all the young boys gathered in the horses and hooked them up to the travois. All the braves were mounted and watched.

Jim and skip took down their teepee and packed their things on the packhorse, mule and the travois. Soon the whole village was on the move; Skip looked all over for Yahto, but could not see her.

"Let's get moving Skip, you will just have to wait to see Yahto".

Reluctantly Skip mounted the big Red Roan, took the reins of the packhorse pulling the travois, called for dog then followed Big Jim and the mule.

For the five days it took to reach the valley, Skip could not see Yahto, he never saw Dull Knife either, and he should have realized they would be at the front, for their father was the Chief.

When they reached the Valley, Jim told Skip they would keep moving for a few more days to reach the higher valley, where they would set up camp and begin trapping.

"Not till I find Yahto". Skip said.

"I figured you would say that, we will camp with the tribe for one day, and then move on".

Skip dismounted and tied his horse to a scrub bush, with Dog at his heals he started walking around the camp looking for Yahto. One of the old women saw him, and knew who he was looking for; she smiled and pointed towards the front of the village.

"Thank you old one". Then walked to the front of the village, seeing Dull Knife he hurried to him.

"My white brother looks for Yahto".

"Yes my brother, where is she".

Dull Knife smiled and pointed to the left, Skip saw her and his heart skipped a beat.

"Thank you my brother, would it be okay if I go talk to her"? Dull Knife nodded at Skip

While helping her mother put up the teepee, Yahto looked all around for Skip,

"Yahto, he will find you, now do your work", said her mother.

"Yes Mother", but she kept looking for Skip as she worked, then she saw Skip heading for her, with a big smile on her face. She looked towards her mother hopeful she would be spared a minute or two to speak with Skip.

Her mother shook her head, "Go talk, but hurry, we have much work to do".

Skip walked up to her, "Yahto, I must go to the upper valley to trap with Big Jim, If I come back in the spring, after the Rendezvous, will you wait for me".

Yahto smiled, "I wait for Skip".

"Yahto come, much work to do". Yahto heard her mother.

Skip touched her hand, she smiled at Skip then she turned and went to her mother.

Skip walked back over to where Dull Knife was working.

"My brother, do you think your father will let me have Yahto for my wife"

"I am sure he will, but you have to give presents for her, that is our way".

"I have little now but after the trapping season, I will go to the Rendezvous and sell my furs, Will a new rifle and shot be enough for her"?

"My father likes you, so I say yes, but it will have to be a good rifle".

"It will be the best one they have, I must go now, Will my brother come to the upper valley and visit". "That I will do my brother, As Skip turned away, Dull Knife, with a big smile on his face, should I bring Yahto with me?", Skip looked back over his shoulder "That would be nice".

Chapter 15

Before the sun was up, Skip and Jim were packing the mule and horse, "This will be a hard climb Skip".

"Do you think your leg is up to it"?

"Don't you worry about this child, youngster".

It did not take long to see what Jim meant. There was switchback after switchback, climb a hundred feet and go back down fifty, to find a way up again, this they done till almost dark. When they made camp, Skip barely ate he was so tired, and soon was in his robes.

"A bit tired are you youngster"?

Skip never heard him; he was already asleep, with Dog curled up next to him.

Three days later, they came to the upper valley. Skip just looked at the valley with his mouth open, The valley had to be almost a hundred and fifty acres, with large pine and oaks all bordering it. Far across the valley Skip could see deer eating in the meadow, Towards the far left corner was a large stream and pools where the beaver dams were, Just from where he was he counted eight dams.

Skip decided that he wanted to spend the rest of his life here, with Yahto.

"It kind of takes your breath away, don't it youngster"?

"I want to build a cabin and live here forever, Jim".

"Well we can build you and that blue eyed girl one, and then one for me on the far end, but we have to get a lot of plews, so we can stock up provisions, the fur trade will not last forever."

They chose a place down near the stream for camp, after the horses were picketed; Jim went off to hunt, while Skip set up camp. Dog took off to find his own supper, Skip watched Dog bound through the fields, and thought to himself, what a great place to live and raise a family.

It was not too long before Skip heard a shot; he paused from what he was doing, and listened, one shot, looks like Jim got some fresh meat. It was not to long before Jim rode up with a nice young doe across the back of his horse. Jim dismounted and took the doe off the horse and brought it close to the fire, they both began skinning and butchering it, when the butchering was done, Jim put a few choice pieces on a split over the fire for breakfast.

When the meat was cooked they sat around the camp fire ate and talked.

"You know Jim, I'm sure glad I got Dog, he saved my life, but looking at all the trees we will need for two cabins, I sure wish we had my long axe".

"That sure would come in handy youngster, with the trapping and building cabins, we won't have much time.

All day they prepared the camp, drying meat, getting in a supply of firewood, for soon the real cold would be coming, the beaver all ready getting their winter fur. But the pelts would not be prime until June or July. They then turned in for the night.

Dawn came early, after their breakfast they started chopping trees down for the cabins; it was hard work with only the small hatchets. Skip was sorry he had traded his long ax, but he was glad to have dog. They would have to make do with what they have; maybe they could get a better ax at the rendezvous.

Chapter 16

The winter was hard and long, they had one room built for Skip's cabin that was high up on a hill looking over the ponds that were at least a mile away. They both spent the winter in that one room, getting the traps and gear ready for trapping, the time went by fast. The snow was almost gone and the ice was off the ponds.

Tomorrow we will start trapping youngster; we will start at the seventh pond, so we won't have as far to travel back to camp, also we will hunt on the way back from setting our traps".

"Why not the eighth pond", asked Skip?

"We don't want to wipe out the whole valley"

Skip got up from the log he was sitting on, "Well I'm going to hit the robes".

Dawn came way too early for Skip, but he got up, walked down to the creek, washed the sleep from his eyes, and filled the coffee pot with water. When Skip got back to the camp, he saw that Jim had a fire going and was making breakfast.

Jim watched Skip as he approached the camp; he knew what was on Skips mind.

"Boy If you want to marry that girl and bring her here to live, you best keep your mind on what you are doing, there is still a lot of danger out there, Just because we see no sign of Indians don't mean they are not around, and you got bears and mountain lions to watch out for".

Skip came out of his daydream, "Right Jim I'm sorry".

"Don't tell me your sorry, you will be the one who is sorry, now keep your mind on what you are doing, you are going to be alone out there".

Skip packed his belongings on the back of his horse, "I will go up to the seventh pond and work my way back, see you in a few days". Skip hollered for dog and headed for the farthest beaver pond.

Jim watched as Skip headed away, smiled and thought to himself, if I had a son, I would like him to be like him, for Jim loved Skip like a son.

As Skip rode away he heard Jim holler, "Watch your topknot boy".

Without looking back, he raised his hand and hollered, "Keep yours old man".

Skip could not help thinking of Yahto. He knew how she would love the beauty of the valley that would be their home.

Reaching the first pond, he found a place to set his first trap, Dropping the reins on the ground, he grabbed a trap off of the horse, told Dog to stay, for he did not want the smell of the dog near his trap.

Close to the water he cut a stake notched it then put it through the circle of the trap and pounded it into the ground then set the trap just as Jim had shown him, set his float stick with the Beaver sent on it, then splashed water on the ground to remove his smell.

He walked in the water a ways before coming out of the water. His feet were freezing when he got back to his horse and Dog. He picked up the reins, looked all around for any danger and headed for the next pond.

It was and boring and hard work, but he did not have to answer to anyone, and the beauty that was all around him made it all worthwhile, Him and Yhato would raise a family and live out their lives in the valley he hoped.

As he approached the last pond, Dog growled and the hair stood up on the back of his neck.

Skip froze, brought his rifle up and cocked the hammer back and looked all around, a Grizzly and her cub came out of the brush about Sixty yards away, She stood up on her hind legs and gave a loud roar, she must have been ten feet tall. Jim's voice came to him; do not shoot a Grizzly unless it is life or death.

He grabbed Dog by the neck and in a low voice told him no, Then turned and walked slowly back the way he came, looking over his shoulder all the way.

When Skip stopped shaking, he told Dog, that they would make camp a further ways down the pond, away from the berry bushes.

He made a note of that in his mind; never make camp near berry bushes.

When Skip thought he was far enough away from the Grizzly, he made camp, built a small fire and put water on for coffee, when the coffee was done he took out some Jerky, threw a piece to dog, then sat with his back against a tree, ate and watched the sun go down.

Knowing he would get no more food, Dog whined and looked at Skip.

Go on get your own dinner, Dog gave a yelp and bounded off

After the sun went down, Skip got into his robes, before Skip fell asleep; Dog was back and lying next to him.

Chapter 17

Dull Knife sat by his tepee and watched, as Tall Oaks drank the whiskey from the jug, soon he thought the jug would be empty, and Tall Oaks would want more.

Dull Knife never drank the white man's firewater, he saw what it did to his brothers, how they would trade anything for it.

He watched and soon saw the jug was straight up, he knew the jug was empty, Tall Oaks threw the jug away and cursed, for he wanted more.

Dull Knife went into his tepee and came out with a jug, of the firewater that he had traded for, knowing sometime he would make a good trade for it.

He walked over to where Tall oaks, was sitting.

"Is your fire water all gone"? Dull Knife asked

Dull knife looked up, saw the jug, smiled, and reached for the jug.

Dull Knife pulled it back. "Want to trade for fire water"?

"What does Dull Knife want"?

"I will trade jug for long axe".

Tall oaks got up went into his tepee and came out with the long axe, handed it to Dull Knife and took the jug.

Dull Knife smiled, "Good Trade". Then walked back to his tepee, and put the long axe away.

The next morning, he took his bow and quiver full of arrows, and the long ax, then bridled his horse, and walked over to his father's tepee, Yahto was outside starting the morning cook fire.

"Do you have the high moccasins that you made for Skip ready"?

Yahto smiled at her brother, and went into the teepee and came out with a Pair of moccasin boots.

Dull knife looked at the fine pair of boots; they were lined with rabbit fur. He smiled and said". You never made me a fine pair of boots like theses".

"For bringing theses to Skip I will make you a pair".

Dull Knife mounted his horse, smiled at his sister, and rode away, for the higher valley.

The ride to the upper valley was a long and hard ride, for there were many switchbacks, But he would make good time, for he had no packhorses, He made camp for the knight eating some jerky and had a drink from the spring.

The next morning he saw the smoke for Skips and Jims Camp, when he was about two hundred yards from their camp, Dull Knife saw where the tracks of four horses, and where two men had lain watching Skips camp.

One of the horses' tracks was very deep. Dull knife new it was the tracks of the one called Crown and the fat man.

He followed the tracks for about a mile and soon came upon their camp, watching from behind some big trees and brush he saw they were sitting around eating, and drinking, he knew they were up to no good, for all their traps were laying on the ground with the rest of their belongings.

He headed for Skips camp to warn them of the two men, upon reaching the camp, he saw Big Jim standing there with his rifle ready, He waved to Big Jim, Jim saw it was Dull Knife and lowered his rifle and waved him in.

Dull Knife told Jim about the two men. Dull Knife could see Jim was red with rage. Skip will be here in the morning, come sit friend and let's eat. The sun was just going down when they finished eating, Dull knife told Jim he had more to tell, but he would wait for morning so Skip could hear, then they turned in for the night.

Chapter 18

The following morning before sunrise, Skip was up and headed the pond to check his traps, every trap had a Beaver in it, he cleaned each Beaver, and kept the choice pieces of meat then buried the rest. Then headed for his camp, upon reaching his camp, he stopped listened and looked the camp over good, when he was satisfied that all was well he entered the camp, Then packed the mule with his furs and his belongings. "Well Dog, lets head for Jim's camp and see how Jim is doing, he mounted the red roan and at a slow walk headed for the main camp.

About a two hundred yards from the main camp, Skip dismounted, tied the reins around the saddle horn, very quietly he walked to camp, with dog following, Skip had learned to walk without making any noise, due to the training of Dull Knife and the time he spent in the mountains.

When dog saw Jim and Dull Knife, he trotted into camp and sat next to Jim, begging for a piece of bacon.

Big Jim smiled, "You have come a long ways youngster; we never knew you were here till Dog trotted in".

Big Jim and Dull Knife were up before the sun was up; they had coffee on and bacon frying when Dog ran into camp.

Skip had a big smile on his face when he saw Dull Knife, Skip dismounted and took the saddle off his horse and let him go to pasture, he unloaded the mule with the big pack of furs and carried them over to Jim's stack of furs.

Skip walked over to Dull Knife reach out his hand, "Dull Knife it is good to see you". Dull Knife reached out and shook Skip's hand, "It is good to see you my brother".

Skip walked over to the fire, picked up the coffee pot and poured himself, a cup of strong black liquid.

Dull knife handed Skip the long handled ax, Skip smiled. Dull Knife smiled, "I make good trade". He laughed.

Skip Took the long ax and thanked Dull Knife, "This will make are work a lot easier my friend".

Big Jim told Skip to sit, "Dull knife has things to tell us".

"Two men came into our camp, one was the man you called Crown, the other was a big fat man, the one called Crown offered a fine rifle, a horse and other things to my father, He wanted Yahto".

Dull knife could see the anger and worried look on Skips face.

"My father told him Yahto was promised to another, then asked the one called Crown where the other man was, who came to camp and traded with him".

Crown said he went off by himself to trap, my father said, he did not believe him, that he was to leave our village and to not come back, for the next time he saw him he would die.

Skip smiled, "That is good".

"There is more, the two men have been watching your camp for a while now, from the tracks, I can tell one is the big fat man".

Big Jim got to his feet, I am going to find their camp and kill that fat bastard Toomey, and if Crown has any of Sketters things, I will kill him too".

Skip looked up at Jim, "We will kill them together".

"I come too, I see the look in Crowns face, he will try to get my sister, and I cannot let that happen": Said Dull knife

Dog was sniffing the air and was letting out a low whine,

"They could be watching our camp as we speak, it will soon be dark, we will wait till morning, then we will all go a different way, then meet about a mile up the creek at the big rock, then we will find their camp, Toomey is mine". Jim Said.

"And Crown is mine", said Skip.

They finished their dinner and turned in for the night, Skip spent a restless night, he wanted daylight to get here, all he could think of was Crown trying to get Yahto, he was no longer a scared boy, he knew he would kill Crown, when he found him.

Chapter 19

Jim was right; Crown was watching the camp from about two hundred yards away. He could not hear what they were saying, but the way they looked towards his camp, he knew they were going to come for them in the morning. Crown knew it was time to get Toomey and leave the valley.

When he reached the camp, the fire was out. And all the food that was cooking was gone, Toomey had eaten it all, and Toomey was in his robes asleep, he was so disgusted with Toomey he felt like crushing his skull with his tomahawk. But with three men coming after them, he needed Toomey for a little while longer. He had planned on killing Toomey before they went to rendezvous. He did not want anyone to know he was with Toomey, he could make up a story, how Toomey had killed Skinner and that he killed Toomey, after he shot Skinner, his friend and partner, then he could keep all the furs, and with enough money he could buy a lot of goods and buy Yahto.

He walked over to where Toomey was sleeping and gave him a kick; Toomey came awake with a pistol in his hand. "Get up we got to move, they know we are here and they will be coming in the morning".

"What about their furs".

"You can wait and try to get them, but I'm leaving".

Crown watched as Toomey got his fat lazy ass out of his robes, and wondered how a lazy scum like him ever lasted so long in the mountains. "You can wait and try to get them, but I'm leaving".

Crown was all packed and ready, Toomey still was taking his time. "You better get a move on it, I want to be miles from here when they show up, that kid is not a kid anymore, and he is bigger than you with no fat".

"And Big Jim, knows you done in Brownie, He told that boy he would kill you on sight".

"Well I'm not scared of Jim".

"Then you're a big fool, he put a lot of men under, and I'm not going to be one of them, the further I can be away from him the better, besides I got that kid to worry about, he knows I want that good looking Squaw".

They packed up all of the furs they had, most were Sketters, who Crown Killed, they headed for the Green River where the second Rendezvous would be held. The year was 1835.

Chapter 20

They came in from three sides, but they knew the camp was empty before they even got there.

Jim said we could track them, but they had a big head start. We will go back and work on the cabins, we will find Crown and Toomey at the Rendezvous, They mounted up and headed back to their valley, Dull knife, told them he would go back to his village and would see them at the Rendezvous.

'Will Yhato and your father be there"?

Dull knife smiled, "I do not know, that is up to my father, my white brother should keep his mind on being careful. If one thinks of a woman all the time, he gets careless and will end up dead".

Dull Knife mounted his horse and rode away.

Skip and Jim packed up all their belongings turned in for the night and would leave in the morning.

When morning came Skip was the first to rise, taking his rifle and pistols with him, he gathered wood for the morning fire, returning back to the camp, he noticed Jim was still asleep in his robe, He gave a chuckle for he knew Jim was awake, and was just waiting for him to get breakfast ready.

Skip put the coffee on the fire and whipped up some batter for hot cakes, when the coffee and flap Jacks were ready Jim rolled out of his robe.

"Is it morning already Skip?"

Skip laughed, "As if you didn't know".

Jim got his cup and plate from his pack and started devouring the flapjacks.

"Skip instead of heading back to the valley, I think we should head for the Rendezvous, we can take our time and do some trapping along the way, I want to be there before Toomey and Crown get there". Skip agreed, cleaned up the two tin plates, they packed their belongings and headed for the Green River Rendezvous.

Chapter 21

They came to the Green river early in the day, stopping at the bank of the river, they looked the campsite over, Jim was amazed at the size of it, far to the left he saw many teepees, he could tell they were different tribes for they were not all together.

"Jim how many tribes are here"? "By the looks of things there are about a half a dozen or so, you see the far one, they are Blackfeet, though there is no fighting between the Indians and us, never trust the Blackfeet, they hate all white men".

They kicked their horses and move across the shallow river. "I usually camp alongside Big Red and Carter, all three of us came to the mountains together with Kit Carson, when we were young men, and they will do to ride the river with".

"Just remember you're a greenhorn and will be treated as one, they will ride you and try to get your dander up, but it will all be in fun. The best thing for you to do is keep your mouth shut and your ears open, and you will hear some big yarns, Never call any of them a liar, we all know they are just yarns most of the time".

As they moved along, Skip could not believe what he was seeing, men were drinking, and fighting, having knife-throwing contest and shooting contest. Indians were walking among the white men, even joining in with the trappers. That's when Skip saw this big Indian with his father's watch hanging around his neck. "That's my father's watch that Indian is wearing, he headed his horse towards the Indian. Jim reached over and grabbed the bridle of Skip's horse.

"Don't do anything here Skip, any trouble and they will make you leave".

Skip studied the Indians face, for he did not want to forget it, He would get his father's watch back and kill the Indian, He did not notice the white hair hanging from the Indians belt, if he did nothing could have held him back.

Big Red yelled, "Hey Big Jim, over here".

Looking over to the right, Jim saw Big Red, Carter, and a few others he knew, they reined their horses over to Red's campsite and dismounted. Big red got up off the log he was sitting on. Skip could see why he was called big Red, for he was bigger than Jim and himself and had a huge red beard. Big Red, walked over to Jim and grabbed him in a bear hug, Dog growled and showed his teeth. Skip grabbed dog by the neck, it is ok boy".

"Good to see you still got your topknot Jim, who's the lad you got with you ". Jim introduced Skip to all at the campsite. "We will join you after we take care of the horses".

While they unsaddled the horses, Jim told Skip things he should know. There will be a lot of ribbing, And you have to take the ribbing you will get, it will all be in fun, and you can even fun back with them.

But let no man push you around, or you will lose respect, and if you get in any fights, and someone pulls a knife on you, then you fight to win, and kill him if you have too.

After the horses were taken care of, they sat at the campsite and the jug was passed around. When it came to Skip, he took a big swallow, It was his first taste of liquor, and he did not expect what he got, he could hardly breath, got all red, and started choking. They all started laughing and big Red slapped him on the back so skip could breath.

"Well it looks like our greenhorn is getting all green". Big Red said. When Skip could breathe again, he laughed with them.

Skip was sitting on a good size flat rock, when a man walked over to the campsite. Hey, Greenhorn you're sitting on my rock. Not wanting any trouble, he started to get up, he saw Jim shake his head no, but he was already up, so he turned and looked at the rock, then he faced the man who was smaller than him. "Is your name ass?"

"What the hell you talking about greenhorn?" asked Clark

Skip smiled at the man, "Well the only thing I see on this rock is a fat ass print, and so if your name is fat ass, I will give up the seat".

All the men gave out a howl and watched to see what would happen.

"Hell no my names not fat ass, now get out of my seat before I spank you"

Skip smiled; you can try if you have a mind too.

Well the man turned as if to go, but then turned and swung a big fist at Skip, but Skip was expecting it, he ducked and came up with a right that landed on the tip of Clark's chin the man hit the ground and was out cold.

Skip sat back down on the rock, and looked at all the men, "Could I try that jug again".

They all gave a howl and passed him the jug. Big Jim smiled; he knew Skip would fit in.

Skip was feeling the effects of the whiskey, he got up went over and spanked the man on the ground a few times, then poured water on the man. They all gave a big laugh. The man came around and sputtered, "What the hell did you hit me with?"

Skip just rubbed his hand; the man walked over to Skip, Skip was ready for another fight.

The man laughed and stuck out his hand, "They call me Clark, You won't be a greenhorn for long, I can tell you that". They all laughed and gave Clark the jug, He took a big long swallow, "maybe this will stop my jaw from hurting, then sat down on the ground, I guess the rock is yours youngster, but you're going to leave a small ass print. They all gave a big laugh.

All through the night they ate buffalo hump, drank, and told yarns, Skip just listened and learned. However, his mind was on that Indian with his father's watch, he was going to keep his eyes on him; he had made up his mind, to get the watch back and kill the Indian, and all that were with him.

The next morning Skip woke up with the biggest headache he ever had in his life. All the same, men were sitting at the campfire as if they never went to sleep. Skip smelled the coffee and meat cooking, the coffee smelled good, but the smell of meat was making him feel sick, He jumped out of his robe and ran behind a tree and puked his guts out. When he came back to the fire, they were all looking at him, but they were not laughing, they had all been through it at one time or another.

"Looks like your greenhorn is a little green this morning, Come and take a swallow from the jug, Greenhorn". Big Red said.

Skip just shook his head, he was afraid to even open his mouth to talk.

Big Red smiled, "Come on youngster, believe me it is the only thing that will help you".

Skip looked over at Big Jim, Jim shook his head yes. Skip walked over to Big Red, took the jug, and took a big swallow, it settled his stomach, so he sat down on his rock, after the way he knocked out Clark, they all figured it should be his rock. Skip took his cup from his possible bag and drank a few cups of coffee; soon his headache was gone.

Big Jim told Skip they would trade in their furs today, and buy what they needed, and then the games would start.

Skip asked, "What games?"

"Oh there will be rifle and pistol shooting, knife throwing, ax throwing and wrestling.

After eating, they got their furs and headed for the trading tables. It was a good time and furs was drawing a good price, seven dollars for prime, and four to five for others. they got close to four hundred dollars each more money than Skip ever saw, but as usual, the prices for the things they needed were high, for they had to be brought in from St Louie a long ways off.

They pooled their money for the things they needed, then with what was left, they bought what they wanted. Skip bought a nice rifle for Yahto's father and a newer cap and ball rifle for himself and three hundred caps, he would keep Brownies old flintlock, for he could always find flint, when he ran out of caps. Then he bought some cloth and ribbons, a small mirror for Yahto. The trader asked if he was going to start a war with the amount of cap's he bought.

Jim asked if Toomey had been in yet. The clerk told him that Toomey and Crown had been in the first day, traded their furs, got supplies and left.

The clerk said, "They had more furs than ever before and they were all prime".

Jim asked if he could see their furs. "That pile right over their".

Jim took a long look at the pile of furs, and right off, he knew they were Sketters. "I'm going to kill both of them the first time I lay eyes on them, these are Sketters furs, and some look like they might be Crowns". Jim asked the clerk if Skeeter has been in yet.

"If he has I have not seen him yet".

When they reached their camp, no one was there; they were all off playing games and drinking.

"Well youngster lets go join n the games". "You go ahead Jim, I'm not in the mood for games, I want to keep an eye on that Indian".

Jim got up and as he was leaving, "You better be careful, that Indian is no one to fool with".

"I'm not going to fool with him, I'm going to kill him, and all that are with him".

"There are woman with him Skip".

"My mother was a woman, and one of them has her locket and her hair pin, they bashed my mother's head in with an ax, then scalped her, and who knows what else they did to her, I'm going to kill every one of them or die trying".

"When you are ready I will go with you".

"No Jim this is something I have to do myself".

Chapter 22

Skip sat on the rock with dog next to him, looking across the creek at the Blackfoot camp, it has been four days at the Rendezvous and trappers and Indians were starting to leave, Skip was not going to lose sight of the big Indian with his father's watch and his Squaw with his mother's broach. He saw no scalps on the Indians belt, but Jim said they would not wear them in camp, for the trappers would get riled and a fight would break out.

Skip never just killed a man or woman that did not try to kill him first, but he wanted to kill them and rip their heart out. he never scalped anyone before But Jim showed him how, For he would carry the mans and woman's scalp with him the rest of his life, And if he found them with his fathers and mothers scalps, He would bury his parents scalps. He did not know he could have so much hate; he had all he could do not to just walk over there and shoot them all right now.

Jim gave him a hard stare, when he asked him to show him how to take a scalp. Jim told him he was taking on a very dangerous thing. Then showed him how to scalp, it did not seem hard to do.

The next morning Skip saw the Blackfeet breaking camp, so he packed what he would need, on his horse. He asked Jim if he would hold on to dog and take his things to the valley.

"Skip I should go with you, they are fighting men you are after".

Skip told him no, this is something he must do alone.

"Well don't you try to be fair and give them any warning, if you are set on this, just shoot them when you have the chance, and make each shot count, and no matter what, don't let them take you alive, and the woman will kill you if they have a chance".

"Skip said he would give them the same chance they gave his Mother and Father, none". He told Jim he was not a Greenhorn anymore and was not a boy".

With his flintlock tied to his saddle, His Hawken cap and ball and two pistols, knife and short ax in his belt, He mounted and followed them.

Crossing the river at its shallowest point, the water was only up to the horses hocks.

Reaching dry ground, He waited and looked around, he did not want to follow to close, looking back across the river, He saw everyone packing up, for the rendezvous' was ending, He saw Jim looking at him, he waved and begin following the Blackfeet.

Somewhere about five miles from the river, he heard a noise behind him, fearing they knew he was following them, Skip turned with my rifle cocked and ready to shoot, then he saw dog, wagging his tail and looking up at him.

"Well dog, you just won't let me out of your sight will you".

Moving slowly along, he started thinking about Yahto, how he wanted to marry her and return to their valley.

Dog was walking in front about ten yards, when he stopped and Skip saw the hair raise up on the back of dogs neck, that's when he realized, if he ever wanted to see her Yahto or their valley again, he better forget both and concentrate on what he was doing.

Skip was climbing a slight knoll when he realized, someone could be on the other side, dog smelled, or heard something. He stopped his horse and dismounted, Then signaled dog to him. Then he got down on his belly, with his rifle out in front of him he crawled to the top of the knoll. Just as he started to look over the knoll Skip came face to face with one of the Indians, the Indian swung his tomahawk at Skips head, Skip rolled over to his right and the tomahawk just missed his head, Skip swung the barrel of his riffle and caught the Indian in the head.

The Indian was stunned but not out of the fight, but had dropped his tomahawk, Skip grabbed the green river knife from his belt and swung it at the Indians neck, he missed by inches, that would have ended it. The Indian pulled his knife out and came at Skip. Skip rose to his feet and met him head on, swinging his knife at Skips chest; he cut Skips deerskin shirt but did not draw blood. They locked hands and fought, trying to stab each other. Skip was much bigger than him, but the brave was strong and very quick, They rolled on the ground both trying to be on top, the Brave got the advantage and was on top of him. Skip had the Indians knife hand in his and he could not stab it into Skip. Then dog grabbed the Indian by the leg and was ripping back and forth with his head and teeth that was all Skip needed. He plunged his knife into the Indians belly and pulled it up till it hit his breastbone, the blade had punctured the Indians heart, Skip then he pulled his knife out and the Brave fell forward, Skip jumped to his feet and was ready for him, but he was done and covered in his own blood. He gave a few kicks then laid still; dog was still chewing on his leg.

Skip walked over to him and rolled him over, and then with his knife he made a circle on the Braves head, grabbed his hair and gave a yank, off came his scalp, his first scalp, and seven to go.

H called dog off him, walked over, and mounted his horse, He knew now that they knew he was following them, he would have to keep his mind on what he was doing, or one of them would be having his scalp in his belt.

He called horse over to him and mounted, then hit his leg and Dog followed, waging his tail, with blood all over his muzzle. The trail was easy to follow, for they were pulling a travois, with their goods on it.

Skip knew there were seven left, so he would make sure he could account for all seven tracks, If he saw less than seven, he would know one or more had dropped back to get him. They were heading west and moving slow. Skip decided to circle around and get in front of them and lay a ambush for them, he wanted to shoot the one who had his father's watch first, but knew he would shoot who ever gave him the best target, man or woman he did not care which one, for he was going to kill them all.

Chapter 23

Crown had traded his furs and bought for guns, powder, shot, and some trinkets, he believed the Shoshone chief would take the guns for Yhato.

Upon reaching the Shoshone village he dismounted on a high knoll and studied the village, before he realized it he was surrounded by Shoshone braves, they took his weapons off him and made him walk to the village.

He protested and told them he brought gifts for the chief, they just pushed him towards village.

When they reached the village they made him sit on the ground and kept two guards on him, He was not worried; he thought the chief would be pleased when he saw the gifts he brought.

They kept him sitting there all day and when night came, they tied his feet and hands; he kept telling them he brought gifts for the chief, but no one would listen, and would not give him food or water.

He was still sleeping when the sun came up, a brave gave him a kick and untied his feet and told him to get up. Then pushed him towards the chief's teepee, when they got to the teepee the brave pushed him to the ground and made him sit there for hours. A squaw came from the teepee and cooked some food, spat at him then went into the teepee. Now he was getting scared.

After what seemed like hours, the chief came out, and looked at him with disgust.

"You were told never to come to our village again, that if you did you would die, do you think I speak with a crocked tongue".

"But I brought you some fine guns to trade for the girl".

The chief shook his head," I told you Yhato is for Cat killer, When my son and Cat killer return we will decide what to do with you, as for the guns, I will keep them and all that you have, for you will not need them. Then he told the brave to take him to a teepee and keep him bound, give him just enough water and food to keep him alive, no more.

"If you let me go, I will never come to your village again".

The chief looked at him with disgust, "I give warning one time, you did not listen, if cat killer say let you go then you can go, if not you die".

Crown had some hope now, he thought a white man would never let them kill him, but then again he was trying to get Skip's woman. Cowards die a thousand deaths, and Crown was a bushwhacking coward, Toomey was no good, but he was not a coward, he was just a ruthless killer and lazy.

It was four days later when Dull Knife rode into camp, the first thing he noticed was Crown tied to a pole in the middle of the village, he rode his horse close to Crown, Crown had to pull his legs in or the horse would have stepped on him.

"You came for my sister, did my father not tell you to never come to our village, if it was up to me, I would bash your head in now".

Dull Knife reined his horse around and went to his father's tepee, dismounted and looked around, seeing his sister coming back from the creek with water. Looking over at Crown, he saw him staring at his sister following her every move; He pulled out his knife and walked over to where Crown was tied to the pole. Crown was so taken with the sight of Yhato, he never heard Dull Knife approach, till he felt the hard kick in his ribs.

"Stupid white man, you were told not to come here. But you come anyways.

Now I tell you, grabbing Crown by the hair, he put the knife blade under Crowns eye, if I see your eyes on my sister one more time, I will cut your eyes out, then he walked to meet his sister, looking back at Crown, he saw Crowns head down"

Chapter 24

Skip kept to the low ground, not wanting to skyline myself, keeping horse at a walk, until he got far enough away from the Indians, then he put the horse into a cantor, until he thought he was far ahead of them, then he looked for a place to set up the ambush.

Skip knew there was a time he never would have thought of killing another human being, but he was so full of hate for the killing of his parents. He thought of what Jim had told me. The Indians ways are so different from ours, anyone who is not of their village is a enemy to them, they do not believe to kill a enemy is wrong, all they know is the white man came to their land and killed their game, took their land, raped their woman and killed their people. They took the furs of their animals, so what is wrong if they took their horses and guns and whatever they could steal from the white man.

Well none of that mattered to me, he would get back what they stole from his parents and take their scalps to wear in his belt for the rest of his life, he must revenge his mother and father's death, at all cost, does not the Bible say an eye for an eye and a tooth for a tooth. Skip knew in his heart that he was just trying to justify what he was going to do. The hate was so great within him that nothing could change his mind.

Skip knew it would be hours before they came into range for him to shoot, so he unsaddled Horse and rubbed him down with dry grass, then set the picket rope where horse could eat the rich green grass. Then Skip sat and ate some jerky and gave some to dog, who laid down next to him, and they waited.

Soon he could see them coming, he checked his two rifles and pistols, then saddled Horse. Jim had taught me to be ready for the worse, Horse was the best horse that Dull Knife's father had, he had speed and lots of bottom, It would be hard for any horse the Indians had to catch him, If he had to make a run for it.

Three braves and three squaws left, he would try to take out the Braves first, wanting the one with his Fathers watch. Two braves were on the right of the travois and one on the far side. Using the Hawken first, for it was the more accurate of the two, he wanted to be sure of his first shot, and it was the fastest gun to reload. Raising the Hawken he drew a bead on the closest Brave, pulled back the hammer and pulled the set trigger, then he squeezed the second trigger ever so gentile, The fifty caliber bucked against his shoulder, without looking to see if he hit the brave, he grabbed the flintlock and fired at the second brave. Then reloaded the Hawken, then looked to see what damage he had done, both braves were down on the ground, the last one was riding away, with his Squaw on the back of the horse with him.

He reloaded the two rifles, then mounted Horse and rode down to the hill to where the braves were laying in the dirt, both squaws were leaning over their men and moaning, they both had knives in their hands. When he was within twenty feet of them, Skip took out his pistols, He aimed at the first squaw, she showed no fear, he could see the sadness and hate in her eyes.

He thought he could shoot them without giving it a second thought. It is one thing to shoot someone from a distance, but another thing to shoot a woman who is looking at you.

The watch was not on either of the dead braves.

Skip looked at the two women, "Do you understand English"?

One of them nodded yes.

"Go, tell your people, I will keep killing every Blackfeet I see till I get my Fathers watch and my Mother's brooch back, and I kill the brave who holds it, do you understand"?

The older squaw nodded her head yes.

"Then go".

He knew the brave he wanted to kill was too far away for him to catch, so he turned horse away from them, called dog and headed back to the Shoshone village. Some of the hate was gone and he was feeling a little sick over killing the other squaws, And he wanted to see Yhato and take her for his wife and go to their valley.

It was a good five or six days back to the village. The weather was cold for winter would soon be here. He was thinking of Yahto, and not paying attention to his surroundings, when an arrow clipped his shoulder. Rolling off horse and dropping his rifle, Skip came up with his pistol. The brave was charging him when he shot him in the chest, the brave fell back and did not move, walking over to him with his knife in his hand, and was ready to scalp him, then changed his mind, no more scalps, except for the brave with the watch.

Now it had started, not only was he hunting them, they were hunting him also, and where was dog, off hunting he guessed, Skip was counting on dog or horse too much.

He could hear Jims voice in his head, get careless out there and you will die. Well he came real close this time, Jim was right he should have let it go, killing the brave would not bring his parents back, what kind of a life would he have with Yahto, having to worry if they would find the valley and kill her and him. Well what's done is done; there is no going back now.

Heading for the village, he heard dog coming, for all of his senses were alert now, no more daydreaming; he did not want the brave wearing his scalp along with his father's watch.

Chapter 25

Toomey had been watching the village for a few days, waiting for a chance to get Crown loose, not that he was a good friend, it was easier to rob and kill when you had a partner. He noticed a tall Indian, who liked his spirits, he would try to find him alone and offer him some rotgut whiskey, to free Crown.

The following day he saw the tall Indian walk into the woods with a jug in his hand, he followed him into the pines, being very quiet he followed and watched as Tall Oaks drink from the jug, after awhile, with a grunt Tall Oaks threw the jug against a tree, it shattered. Toomey knew this was the time to make his move, he moved out from the tree he was hiding behind.

Tall Oaks was not that drunk yet, for he only had a little in his jug, He got up with a tomahawk in his hand, glaring at Toomey.

"Easy my friend, as he raised the jug, I thought you might like a drink with me".

Tall Oaks smiled and reached for the jug, Toomey was no fool; this jug only had a few swallows in it. Tall Oaks drank what was in the jug.

"Why you come with so little?"

"Oh I have more my friend".

"Let us drink it".

"Not so fast, I have a friend in your village, you get him free, and I will give you a full jug".

Tall Oaks had his tomahawk in his hand. He got up threaten with his tomahawk: "You get now".

Toomey pointed his pistol, "You bring my friend here when it is dark and you get the jug and no tricks, I will be watching you". Then he got up keeping Tall Oaks covered with his pistol, and moved off into the pines.

Keeping out of sight, Toomey watched the village all day, when night time came, he moved off to where he had told Tall Oaks to meet him with Crown, he had no more whiskey, so he filled the jug with water, he knew he would have to kill the Indian.

Hiding in the brush, he heard them coming, Tall Oaks had Crown with him, but Crown still had his hands tied behind him.

Toomey stepped out from behind the brush, with the jug in his hand, "Untie my friend".

"You give jug then you get friend".

Crown reached the jug out to Tall Oaks, Tall Oaks only had eyes for the jug; he did not see the tomahawk in Toomey's hand.

Tall Oaks took the jug and raised it too his lips, one swallow and he knew he was tricked, when he lowered the jug, Toomey swung the tomahawk and split Tall Oaks's head open, he then untied Crown and they took off into the pines.

"I would like to go back for that young squaw."

"Are you nuts, I did not risk my live so you could get some Indian girl, you try to go back, and I will kill you myself"?

"We got work to do, Big Jim and that kid is looking for us, and they will kill us on sight, we are going to wait till they get a nice pack of plews, then kill both of them, who knows maybe the girl will be with them, I have not been with a young squaw in a long time".

Crown thought to himself, you will never have her, she is going to be mine and mine alone, and I will kill you if you try to touch her.

Chapter 26

SKIP ASKS FOR YHATO

Upon reaching the Shoshone village, Skip was met by his friend and blood brother Dull Knife,

"It is good to see my brother; you are no longer that scared boy I met long ago, I see you still have dog".

As they greeted each other, Dull knife told him that Crown was there and tried to trade for Yhato.

"Where is he I am going to end his life".

"He is gone, My father kept him as a prisoner waiting for you to come, But Tall Oaks freed him. I followed his tracks, and found Tall Oaks, with his head bashed in, the tracks told me that a big heavy man was there waiting and killed Tall Oaks. there was a whiskey jug next to Tall Oaks, he must have freed Crown for a jug of whiskey, but it seems Toomey killed him and freed Crown, they left together, that was a few days ago.

"I have brought presents for your father and will ask for Yhato to be my wife".

"My father knows you will ask for her, and will take whatever you have for her, he will be happy for you to take Yhato for your wife, but do not ask for her today unless my father says it first, it is custom to visit with my family for a few days first".

Skip dismounted, A young boy came and took skips horse, skip told him thanks and walked with Dull Knife to his father's teepee. a few dogs came growling after dog, dog met them head on and after a brief fight the two dogs ran off torn and bleeding with their tails between their legs, Neither Skip nor Dull Knife paid any attention. That was the way in a Indian camp, survival of the fittest.

When they reached Black Hawks teepee the flap was open, this meant anyone could enter, if the flap was closed then you had to make a scratching sound on the flap, then if the owner wanted he would let you in.

Dull Knife entered his father's teepee with Skip behind him, seated by a small fire sat Black Hawk, and his wife, he motioned for them to be seated, they both sat to the left of the Chief. Both waited for the elder to speak first.

"It is good to see my white son".

"And it is good to see my Father and Mother".

Skip opened his possible bag and took out a knife that he handed to Black Hawk and some beads to his Indian mother who gave Skip a big smile.

Black Hawk nodded and lit his pipe, he took a few puffs and handed it to Skip, with a smile on his face, for he knew, it always made skip cough. too Black Hawks surprise, Skip took the pipe drew in some smoke and exhaled without coughing, Black Hawk smiled and took the pipe back, Skip reached in his bag and took out a pipe, all laughed.

'I see my young son has his own pipe now".

Skip nodded and smiled, for the joke was on Black Hawk this time, and the chief always liked a good joke, even if it was played on him.

They talked of what had happened since they last saw each other.

"You will have to kill this Crown, for he wants Yhato more than anything".

Skip nodded, "When we meet he will die, this I promise you".

"This Crown is bad for Indians and white men, it will be good when he no longer walks the earth, and then your wife will be safe".

Skip gave a big smile, for he knows now that Yhato will be his wife, Now that Black Hawk brought the subject up it was okay for skip to ask for Yhato to be his wife.

"I would be happy if Black Hawk would let Yhato be my wife, I have a very nice gift for you, I will get it now if it is okay".

Black Hawk nodded, Skip got up and went out of the teepee and got the Hawken rifle, along with caps, powder and balls.

When he entered the teepee, he could see the pleased look on Black Hawks face.

This is a fine present you give to me and I will be pleased for Yhato to be your wife.

Skip was grinning from ear to ear, for this is the day he has been waiting for.

Skip thanked the chief for his daughters hand and left the teepee. Once outside he looked around for Dull Knife, he asked a young brave if he knew where Dull Knife was, the brave pointed towards the horse herd.

Skip walked to the horse herd and found Dull Knife working with a beautiful pinto horse.

"My brother looks very happy, did my Father give permission for you to court Yhato".

Skip gave a big smile.

"Yes he did".

Then Skips smile disappeared. "What if she doesn't want me"?

Dull Knife laughed, "Do not worry about that my brother, she wants you".

"Well how do I ask her to be my wife"?

"You have to take the blanket walk, so the village will know that you and her will be married".

"What is a blanket walk"?

"Well my brother, you get your best blanket and go to my father's tepee, If Yhato wants to be your wife she will come out and get under the blanket with you, then you two walk around the village for all to see".

Skip got his best blanket and walked over to the Chiefs teepee, he was so nervous that his knees were shaking. It seemed like he was waiting outside the tepee for hours and he thought she did not want him. Just as he was going to walk away, Yhato came out of the tepee and looked at Skip with a big smile on her face. Skip opened the blanket and Yhato got under the blanket with him, as they walked around the village, Skip asked when they could get married, Yhato told him, in four days, it will be a full moon, they would marry then.

Skip gave a big smile, and then said.

"I can't get married without Big Jim here".

"We will ask one of the young boys to go get Big Jim'.

They walked around the whole village a few times, then Yhato said she had to go back to the teepee, when they reached the tepee Skip gave her a big kiss, and did not like letting her go. Yhato looked back smiled and went into the teepee.

Skip walked back to the horse herd where Dull Knife was, when he reached Dull knife he asked what will he do for four days.

Dull Knife laughed and said we can go hunting; I know where a small herd of Buffalo are, it will take a day and a half to get there and the same back, we will be back just in time for the wedding, a nice fat Buffalo cow will be nice for the wedding feast. Skip said that will be good and gave a whistle for Horse.

"Dull Knife, I don't know where my belongings are".

Dull Knife pointed to a tepee that was all by itself.

"They are in the wedding tepee where you will spend your first night with Yhato".

"I will get my things, and we can hunt towards my valley and meet Big Jim on the way".

Horse followed Skip as he walked to the teepee. When he reached the tepee, he noticed all the young girls looking at him and giggling, his face turned red and he went into the teepee and got his belongings. when he came out of the teepee, the young girls were still there giggling and looking at him, he saddled horse, the young girls were still watching him and giggling, he hurried and mounted Horse and went to meet Dull Knife. Before he reached Dull Knife, Dog was by his side; Dull Knife was mounted and had Skip's mules with him.

"It is good you brought your Bow, we will not use your gun today, and we will get two cows the old way, Skip nodded.

As they headed to the open prairie, Dull Knife told Skip, "You must keep your mind on what you are doing,

Buffalo can be very dangerous, I don't want to tell my sister her man is dead before she is married.

"Well my brother I don't want you to ever have to tell her that I am dead".

"Then keep your mind on the hunt and not your wedding night". Then Dull Knife gave a chuckle. When they reached the small heard, Dull Knife pointed to two cows a little off to the side.

"We will kill those two, they have no calves".

They both gave a holler and headed for the two cows; Horse was much faster than the pinto so Skip reached his cow first. With an arrow already notched aiming just behind the cows leg he let the arrow fly, the arrow entered just behind the cows leg and into her heart, the cow ran for another fifty yards then dropped to its knees then fell over, the cow gave a few kicks then laid still. Skip looked for Dull Knife, he spotted him about twenty yards away skinning out his Buffalo, he did not see the bull that was charging him. Skip took his rifle off his horse and cocked the rifle and aimed at the bull, as he was aiming Dull knife happened to look up at Skip, seeing the rifle aimed in his direction he got scared and raised his hands, Just then Skip fired; the bull dropped about ten feet from Dull Knife.

Dull Knife hollered thanks and said, "I guess we will have two cows and a bull".

Skip reloaded his rifle then finished skinning and cutting up his cow.

After they skinned out the other cow and the bull they wrapped the meat in the hides, put them on the two mules, and headed back to camp, when they heard someone holler, they turned and saw Big Jim heading their way.

Jim rode up and said, "I hear we are going to have a wedding, and a nice feast by the look of things."

Skip shook his head, You are always thinking of your belly". They laughed and headed back to the Indian Camp.

Skip asked Dull Knife, "What the wedding would be like".

"It is quite simple my brother, you and Yhato will stand in front of my Father and say some words that I will teach you, then there will be a big feast and then you and Yhato will go to your tepee".

"That is all", asked Skip

Dull Knife laughed, "Unless you need me to tell you what to do in the tepee".

Skip got all red in the face, "To be honest I most likely do, but I will manage on my own".

On the ride, back to camp Dull Knife taught Skip the words he would have to say at the wedding ceremony.

Chapter 27

THE WEDDING

That night Skip lay alone in the tepee that would soon be Yahto's and his. Jim was in the other tepee that they use to share.

Skip went over and over the words he would have to say, then his mind drifted back to his mom and dad, He thought of how his mother had taught him to read from the family Bible, he was sad that the Bible had perished in the Indian attack.

Thinking of all the work he and his father had done in the fields, just trying to hack out a life, and for what, in just a few minutes the Indians had taken a life's work away, along with the only family he had. Then he thought of Yhato and the family they would have, he vowed to himself no one would ever harm Yhato while he lived. Then finally going over the words he would have to say sleep over took him.

The next morning as the sun was just rising, Skip put some wood on the coals, for the morning was cold. Taking his guns and possibles bag, he walked down to the river, with Dog following him. the village was rising also, women were gathering wood to cook the morning meal, they would smile as skip walked by and he would nod hello to them, thinking to himself, he never thought the Indians were people just like him, they loved their children, played games just like white people.

When he reached, the river he looked all around making sure it was safe, then laid his guns down, took off his clothes and plunged into the freezing cold water. He called for Dog to come in, all Dog did was whine; no way was that dog was going in the water. The water was too cold to stay in very long, so he swam to the shore and got dressed, Dog walked over to him whining, so Skip petted his head, then grabbed him and threw him in the river.

"That should kill the fleas and get rid of your stink, then laughed as dog whined and came back to the shore, shaking the water off. Skip walked towards Dog to pet him; Dog gave a growl and ran off.

Skip walked back to the village, he looked over at the chief's tepee, hoping to see Yhato, but it was Yahto's mother who was gathering the wood, she looked at skip smiled and shook her head, you cannot see her till it is time for the wedding. Skip smiled and walked back to his tepee.

Inside the teepee, he took a Beaver pelt from his pack and opened it, inside was a beautiful red scarf, a pack of needles, two spools of thread and a small pack of colored beads. A present for his bride to be, he hoped it would be enough and she would like them.

The coals were still hot, so he put some wood on the coals and took some Buffalo steaks from the Buffalo hide and put them on a spit to cook.

The meat was about half cooked when there was a scratching at the tepee entrance, Skip said to enter, Big Jim walked in.

"What you cooking there Skip"?

"I swear you can smell food a mile away, have a seat and let's eat".

Big Jim sat down and took out his knife and stabbed a piece of meat, that was half cooked,

"Are you trying to ruin that meat boy"?

"I don't think you even need a fire to cook meat, you would probably take a bite out of a living Buffalo".

"Stop your jawing and eat, it is almost time for you to get married.

They sat around talking for a few hours, and then Dull Knife came and got them for the wedding.

In the center of the village, there was a big fire with huge Buffalo roast cooking and the whole village was there.

Skip looked for Yhato, but could not see her. Dull Knife told Skip to sit on a pile of Buffalo robes, As Skip sat on the robes, he saw Yhato coming to him. She had on a beautiful white Deer skin dress, he thought he never saw anyone so beautiful, when she got to him, skip got up and took her hand, then Yhato led him to where her mother and father were standing.

Black Hawk looked at Skip "What do you have to say to my daughter Skip"?

Skip cleared his throat, and with a quivering voice looked at Yhato and said.

O' my beloved, our love has become firm by your walking as one with me. Together we will share the responsibilities of the lodge, food, and children. May the

Creator bless us with noble children to share? May they live long?

Yhato looked into Skips eyes and with a strong voice said.

This is my commitment to you, my husband to be. Together we will share the responsibility of the home, food, and children. I promise that I shall discharge all my share of the responsibilities for the welfare of the family and the children.

The Chief looked at Skip.

"I give to you my daughter, and in the eyes of the people of my village you are now a Shoshone, now we will feast".

The whole village gave a big roar, and the feast began. It seemed to Skip that the feast would never end, hours later Yhato took his hand and led them to their teepee, a large group of young people followed, they were in the teepee for a little while, when small stones kept hitting the teepee and they could hear giggling outside.

Skip asked Yhato if they were going to stay and do that all night.

"Let them stay for a few minutes, then go out and let out a big roar and the children will run away.

Skip laughed and gave Yhato a big hug and a kiss, then he went out of the teepee spread his long arms as far as he could, then gave out a big roar, the children laughed and run away.

Then skip took his new wife and got under the robes with her.

The next morning, along with Big Jim they headed for their valley and new home.

Chapter 28

It was hard to believe that he had been married to Yahto for two years and she was getting ready to have his child, he was hoping it would be a boy, as all men wish to have the first born a boy.

The cabin They had lived in for two years had two rooms, one to live in and one to sleep, it was nothing fancy, but it was built snug and warm. With the baby coming, Skip new it would need another room, big Jim who lived at the other end of the valley, would help him. after the child is born they will start cutting logs for the other room, as of right now Skip was afraid to leave Yahto alone for too long or stray out of earshot of the cabin. Yahto smiled at him when she saw how he was acting, she told him not to worry, that Indian women have been having their children alone for a long time.

Skip had been mending the corral all day. with his pistol in his belt and hi rifle leaning against the pole next to him, when he heard a baby cry. Skip dropped what he was doing, grabbed his rifle and ran to the cabin, almost knocking the door off the hinges, he ran into the room and to her, she looked like she was still in a lot of pain, as she handed him the baby, it's a girl she whispered through gritted teeth. She had light hair like my mother, Skip was not disappointed that it was a girl, for she was beautiful. Then to his surprise, Yahto gasped and said "There is another one to come".

Skip just stood there with his mouth open, holding his little daughter, not knowing what to do. He could see Yahto was in pain and pushing hard, and before Skip put the baby in her crib and helped, with the second baby that was coming, this one was big, he knew it had to be a boy. He had dark hair and darker skin, so there Skip stood a girl in the crib and a boy in his arms. He looked at Yahto smiled and told her, we are going to need a bigger cabin, maybe two more rooms. Skip cleaned up both babies as best he could, then cut a blanket in half, wrapped them one in each and gave them both to Yahto. He was so happy, proud, and full of himself. grabbing his rifle, ran outside and fired a shot in the air, knowing this would bring Big Jim over. telling Yhato, that he would like to name the girl after his mother, Eileen Janet Sullivan. The boy they would have to think on, for he wanted a strong name for him. It was a long and stressful day for all of them. Soon all four were asleep.

Just as the sun was rising, Big Jim rode in at a gallop. Skip heard him coming and was waiting on the porch for him, with a the big smile on his face.

"Am I an uncle, is it a boy?"

Skip told him he was and uncle, and that it was a boy and a girl.

Big Jim let out a holler, "Skip you're going to need a bigger cabin".

They both laughed, Skip told him the girl would be called Eileen Janet Sullivan, after His Mother, the boy he was not sure yet, and would have to think on it.

"Well Skip, you are real good at names, let's see, we have dog and horse, why not just boy". Then he laughed, Skip just shook his head, no, I will give him a good strong name.

It would take most of the summer and the winter to build the extra rooms on the cabin, but they still had to trap, for they would need supplies to help them through the winter.

Skip was afraid to leave Yhato and the children alone, so for the next two weeks he stayed around the cabin, working on the corral and chopping wood for the winter. The following morning when he woke up, Yahto was already up and had coffee and flap jacks ready, he was glad that Jim showed her how to make them, for they were his favorite. After eating, he went out to chop wood, as while Skip was chopping wood Jim rode up. Dismounting and tying his horse to a pole on the porch, Jim walked over to him and looked up at him, "Boy we have got to start trapping".

Skip thought it was funny Jim looking up at him and calling him boy, Jim was a big man well over six feet, but he still had to look up at Skip for Skip was six five or so.

"I figured you would be here any day now, and I know you are right, but I fear to leave my family alone".

"Skip, you showed her how to use a rifle and pistol, she is an Indian, and knows how to watch out for herself, we need furs so we can get supplies, now get ready and lets go".

Knowing Jim was right, he went into the cabin and told Yahto, to keep both guns loaded and the pistol on her at all times, They had plenty of venison and supplies to last for the month they would be gone. Kissing Yahto and the children goodbye, he walked out of the cabin. Jim had his horse and the packhorses ready to go. He could see dog was all excited and ready to go, dog did not look happy when he was told "not this time dog, you need to stay and look after our family".

As They rode away, Skip looked back and saw Yahto wave to them from the cabin doorway, then they headed for the ponds and their trapping camp. It was a easy ride to the ponds and their Trapping camp.

Reaching the ponds, They made camp. They were about five miles from Skip's cabin and about a half a mile from the first beaver pond. With the horses picketed in some lush green grass and close to a small stream, Jim and Skip headed up the creek to the ponds, Jim stopped at the third pond and would trap back towards their camp. Skip would start at the seventh pond and work his way back to camp.

The day was hot and sunny, not a cloud in the sky, as Skip headed for the eighth pond, looking all around and listing for danger, no more being careless, he had three people depending on Him. As he walked over to the stream and knelt down for a drink, as he cupped the water in his hands, he saw something very shinny glistening in the water, He picked it up and took a good look at it. Though Skip had never seen Gold before, he knew it was a Gold nugget, it was about the size of the tip of his small finger, it was very heavy for its size. looking around he found four more about the same size; he put them in his possibles bag and took a good bearing on where he was then headed down to the pond to set his traps.

As each trap was set in the ice-cold water, he kept a good lookout for any danger, for the Blackfeet were hunting him as well as he was hunting them.

Normally we would make our own camps then meet when we had a good supply of plews, but Skip wanted to show Jim what he had found, he mounted horse and led the packhorse back to Jim's camp.

Upon reaching the camp Skip hollered out, "Hello the camp".

"Come on boy, I heard you coming a mile away".

Skip knew he never heard him till he was close to the camp, but Jim would never admit that.

"What brings you back so soon, the trapping is never that good".

He walked over to the fire where Jim was sitting and drinking coffee, grabbed his cup and filled it with the mud that Jim called coffee and sat down on a log next to the fire.

He reached into his possibles bag, pulled out the small pouch, tossed it to Jim, who plucked it out of the air; as he opened the pouch, and poured out the nuggets, his eyes lit up. "where you get these" he exclaimed.

Down near the first pond where the stream comes out from the mountain.

"How much you think they are worth"?

"Well if we could find a few more like these, we would not have to trap this year".

"That sounds good to me; I could stay close to home".

"That would cause a big problem boy, we would have more people in this valley than we want, once they hear of gold no one could keep them out".

"Okay what do we do?"

"I say we trap as normal and look for the gold at the same time. Let's save the gold for when the beaver trade wears out, it won't last forever. If we don't get enough furs to get us through a winter, we can sell some of the gold".

"You just said that would bring a lot of people to our Valley".

"One of us would have to make the trip to St Louis, and trade the gold for supplies there; it would take about a month or so. That way there's less chance of people knowing where we hails from".

"Okay Jim you know more about this stuff than I do, but we may not even find anymore gold".

"That's true, so then we just keep doing what we been doing, one thing we are not going to do is get gold fever, I like the life I been living, a little gold would just make it a bit easier".

Chapter 29

Crown watched the cabin from a distance of about two hundred yards. He watched Skip cut wood and thought of putting a ball in him. Crown raised his rifle to his shoulder and drew a bead on Skips back, for he was a back shooter, he pulled back the hammer; He was just ready to pull the trigger when Big Jim rode into the clearing. He lowered his gun, he would not try shooting Skip now, for he feared Big Jim.

He saw them talking and laughing, then watched as they went into the cabin, He was obsessed with having Yhato, he would hide here all day if he had to. Finally, they came from the cabin, got their horses and mules ready, then mounted and started away, then Yhato came to the door-waving goodbye to Skip. Just seeing her in the door had him breathing heavy, he wanted to hurry down to the cabin and get her, but he knew he had to wait till Skip and Jim got far away.

Yahto was cleaning the cabin and making stew, when she though she heard movement outside. Not one to ever take chances, she walked silently over to the wall and took down the pistol, checking to see if a cap was in place. holding the pistol behind her with the hammer cocked she waited and listened. She heard someone out on the porch, she thought it could be Skip who forgot something, but he would have hollered that it was him. Yahto knew she should have put the bar on the door, but she had not, she lunged for the door to lock it, when the door burst opened and Crown came in.

As he walked for her, he had a big grin on his face, "I told you that you would be mine".

When Crown was about two feet from her she brought the gun around from her back and shot him dead centre in his chest, the fifty-caliber ball drove him back through the open door and out on the porch. Crown reached both hands to his chest, looked at her and then fell over backwards. His feet gave a few jerks then he laid still, as the gates of hell opened for him.

Not taking any chances she went to the wall and got the rifle, she pulled back the hammer and walked out the door, his eyes were open, but she could see they had no life in them. "I told you I would never be yours". She walked back into the cabin and reloaded the pistol she had just shot, for Skip had taught her to always reload.

Yahto went back out to the porch. She walked around Crown and went to the corral, she got her horse and a rope, walked the horse to the cabin, reaching up she put a loop around the horses head and then tied the other end of the rope to Crowns foot, went back into the cabin and got the rifle off the wall. Skip had always warned her never go far from the cabin without the rifle and pistol. Leading the horse she dragged Crown to the trees that were a few hundred yards from the cabin, Yahto took the rope off her horse and untied Crowns foot. Then she took his possibles bag and powder and shot pouch. She looked down at Crown and said, "Now you can join your brother's the coyotes".

She looked around and saw Crowns horse tethered to a nearby tree, she walked over to it, speaking softly so not to frighten the already nervous animal, she led both horses back to the corral. Yahto took the bridle and saddle off Crowns horse and draped it over the rails of the corral, picking up his rifle and pack she headed to the cabin. She left his pack out on the porch; she brought the rifle into the cabin and placed it near the door. She hoped Skip had heard the shot and would come back. She put the bar on the door and went back to her chores.

Chapter 30

The month or so they had spent trapping and looking for gold, seemed like a year to Skip, for he wanted to get back to his wife and children.

They had, a good month, and got a lot of furs, not as much as they needed, but they had found a lot of gold, and knew there was more to be found, but they were happy living in their valley up in the mountains, and had no dreams of being rich.

Skip and Big Jim sat around the campfire, drinking coffee and eating. Skip was in a quiet thoughtful mood. Big Jim looked over at Skip and asked what was wrong, as if he did not know that Skip was missing his wife and children.

"I was thinking, that maybe I would not go to rendezvous this year, if you would not mind taking the furs and getting the supplies, I would not enjoy it so much this year.

"I had a feeling you would not want to go, I will miss not having you with me, but I understand, I have made the trip alone before".

"Thanks for understanding Jim".

"Well Skip, you have been like a son to me, and Yhato and the kids are like my family".

"Jim, you have been more like a father to me than my own was, and yes we are your family".

Big Jim smiled and said; well let's turn in, we can pack up in the morning and head for home, when we get there I will rest my horse and Sara and then head for St Louis. I most likely will be gone three to four weeks.

"That sounds good Jim, I will do some work on your cabin while you are gone".

They both turned into their robes and went to sleep.

Skip had a restless night for he was in a hurry to get started for home.

Skip was up before first light and had everything packed and waiting, He had coffee, sourdough bread and bacon ready to eat. He nudged his friend with his foot, "Chow time"

Big Jim rolled out of his robe and said "seems you are in a hurry to get home boy, well let's eat and be on our way, I kind of like when you're in a hurry, less for me to do". har har.

After they ate, Big Jim and Skip headed for home with Skip in the lead.

Chapter 31

They camped close to the stream where Skip had found the Gold, The next morning Big Jim was packed and ready to go.

"Boy, you pay attention now, don't be dreaming of Yhato and the kids, those Blackfeet may be watching for you".

"And you do the same old man." Then he laughed.

Skip could hear Big Jim mumbling as he rode away, old man am I, darn come to think of it, I am an old man, then he laughed.

Skip spent the rest of the day panning for gold, he had a little luck and found a few nuggets, then ate his dinner and turned in for the night.

Getting an early start, Skip though he might get home before dark, going up and down the switchbacks took a long time, but that's what made the valley hard to find. Dusk came upon him faster than he liked, and he had to make camp for the night. he unsaddled his horse and ground hitched him near a small stream and good grass, then started a small fire and made coffee, while the coffee was making he took a good look around to make sure he was alone, it was best to play it safe.

He poured himself a cup of coffee and ate some of the bacon and bread left over from morning, He looked over at dog, "I should not give you anything to eat, you were suppose to stay home with Yhato "He threw a few pieces and a bisque to dog, for he wanted dog to stay close tonight. then he turned in for the night.

Skip was up and on his way at first light, not even making coffee, dog looked at him and whined. Skip looked at dog, "You will eat when we get home, a few hours without food won't kill you".

As they reached the top of the mountain and his valley, he could see vultures circling around where his cabin was. He gigged the big black and headed for his cabin on the run, when he got close, he checked his rifle and put it on full cock. Then looked all around for trouble, all looked okay, smoke was coming from the chimney and the horses were in the corral. then he noticed a strange horse, when he got close to the cabin he called out to Yhato, she opened the door and gave him a big smile, Skip smiled back and knew all was okay.

He dismounted and gave Yhato a big hug and a kiss. "I saw the vultures and got scared for you.

"All is okay my husband, I did have a visitor, that English man showed up and barged into the cabin, I had to shoot him, then I dragged him away from the cabin, let the vultures have him, they need to eat too".

Skip nodded and they went into the cabin, Skip went over to his children, picked them both up and just stared at their faces, he never knew he could love anybody so much.

Yahto prepared dinner, they ate and Skip told her of the gold they had found, then they turned in for the night.

Chapter 32

Skip woke up and went outside, there hanging from the porch was his father's watch, A old scalp, not his fathers, it was black, some beads and a broken arrow, he did not know what to make of them, he would have to ask Jim or Dull Knife what they meant. He did understand what was meant by giving the watch back to him, The Blackfeet wanted him to stop hunting them. Skip left everything the way they were, for Jim or Dull Knife to see. He got the water pail and walked down to the lake, rifle in hand, for this whole thing could be a Blackfoot trick, dog came out of the woods and followed him to the lake, Skip always felt better when dog was with him, dog would know if anyone was around before him.

After filling the bucket, and looking all around, everything seemed to be alright, the birds were singing and the squirrels were playing grab ass, so he headed back to the cabin to chop some wood for the morning breakfast, Blue would be up by now, He started calling Yahto Blue, for it was easier to say.

By the time he got back to the cabin Jim was there, He loved the flap Jacks Blue would make, he was not one to ever pass up Blues flapjacks.

Skip smile at Jim, "I thought you would be on your way to St Louie", not that he cared, that Jim stopped over for breakfast, chances are he would not have lived long without Jim, and besides Jim was family, he was like a father to him and Blue.

Jim was looking at the things the Blackfoot brave had left. Skip asked him what they meant. Jim told him, it was clear they did not want you to hunt them anymore, the beads mean he traded for the watch, and the scalp means he did not kill the owner of the watch, the arrow is a Ute arrow and that's who he traded with for the watch.

"Boy you have a reputation of one not to mess with, but don't think he is afraid of you, now can we get some flapjacks, I'm hungry".

Skip laughed and asked him when was he not hungry. Then they went into the cabin, Blue was whipping up the flapjack batter, so Skip started the fire and put the coffee on. After breakfast, Skip told Big Jim he was going to ride down a ways with him and pan a little more for gold. They packed all the furs and gold and headed down the mountain.

Chapter 33

TRIP TO ST LOUIS

Big Jim had told skip it would take him about a month if all went well, three weeks later he pulled into St Louis; he knew he had a small fortune of gold with him, about eight ponds of gold nuggets.

As he entered the city, he could smell the stench of the city, he could not understand why anyone would want to live in such a place, talking to his mule like mountain men did, Sara, that's what he called her, There must be at least two thousand people in this place.

The first thing he did was head for the assayer's office to see how much he would get for the gold. He pulled up to the hitching rail and tied up his horse and mule, two rough looking men were sitting in chairs on the porch of the assayers office, they were looking him over as he took the large bag off the mule, he nodded to them as he went in.

The clerk asked what he could do for him. Big Jim asked what the going price for Gold was. The assayer asked if he had Gold, Jim said I asked what the price was for Gold.

The clerk told him it was $18.83 cents an ounce. Jim told him, to let him have a weighing pan then dumped the gold from his bag in the pan.

The clerk said it looked like he did good and asked where the strike was, Big Jim said now wouldn't you just like to know that?, Just weigh it up and keep your hands away from the scale.

The clerk gave Jim a dirty look, "Not very trusting are you old timer".

Jim smiled. "That's how I got to be an old timer, now how much does it all weigh"?

"Looks like you got seven pounds and six ounces; at $18.83 an ounce you got a small fortune here".

Jim took a pencil and piece of paper off the desk and figured out how much he had coming.

"You owe me $2,108.96 cents".

The clerk figured it out and said that's right, "I will make you out a bank draft".

"The hell you will, I want Gold coins".

"Old Timer I don't have that much gold coins here, just take the bank draft down the street to the bank and they will give you Gold or paper money, or whatever you want".

"Ok give me the Bank draft, and it better be good, you don't want me to come back after you".

Jim took the draft note and walked out the door, the two men were still sitting there.

One asked if he struck it rich.

"No not really. Just a few nuggets, I make more money selling the guns and horses from the men that follow me when I leave town".

Jim took his horse and mule and walked down to the bank. He tied the mule and horse to the hitching rail and went into the bank, and gave the casher the bank note.

The cashier asked how he wanted the money.

Jim put a rawhide pouch on the counter and told the cashier. "Give me ninety-five, 20 dollar Gold coins and the rest in paper". The bag weighed close to six pounds, Jim like the weight of it and smiled as he left the bank.

Jim looked up the street to the assayer's office, the two men were still sitting there, but now there was two horses tied to the hitch rail.

Well Sara, looks like them guys don't take good advice, well we can always use a few more guns and horses. Jim looked up and down the street, looking for a place to buy the supplies they needed. His eyes fell on the big sign, Preston's Mercantile.

He would have to walk past the two men sitting in front of the assayer's office, without looking at the two men, he looked at their horses and saw they each had a flintlock rife on their horses. He muttered, dang I was hoping they would have the new Hawkins cap and ball, well I could always sell them at the next Rendezvous.

Jim entered the mercantile and took out his list.

The clerk asked if he could help him, Jim said, I hope you got all I need; the clerk said I am sure I can fix you up with what you need.

Then Jim started reading off his list, let's have ten pounds of coffee, a sack of flower, two pounds of salt, two pounds of sugar and three ponds of tobacco.

The clerk gave him a big smile and started filling the order. Jim said before you fill the order let's see one of the new Hawken rifles.

The clerk took one of the Hawkins down from the shelf; I just might close early today, as he handed the Rifle to Jim.

Jim marveled over the workmanship of the rifle, the fine walnut stock, the octagon barrel. How much he asked the clerk, "One hundred dollars and you get a hundred caps and balls with it".

"Why that's more than twice the price of a flintlock".

Yes said the clerk, "But it's twice the rifle".

"Do they misfire much".

"To be honest mister I never fried one, but I hear they are more reliable than a flintlock, why they say it will fire even in the worst rainstorm, no primer to get wet".

Still looking at the rifle, Jim said, double the caps, balls, and I will take two.

The clerk wanted to make the sale, but wanted to make a good profit.

"I can double the caps but not the balls"

Jim started to hand the rifle back, then the clerk said: "I can throw in two bars of lead and a mold".

Jim smiled, "Ok I will take two rifles with double caps and double the lead and two molds.

Deal said the clerk.

When the order was filled, Jim and the clerk loaded the order on the mule, and then went back inside for the guns; Jim loaded both rifles, and then said I want two yards of that yellow cloth and some of those beads, and two sewing needles. He almost forgot the things Skip wanted for Yhato.

The clerk said that's a lot for one mule to carry.

Jim said he was going to get a few pack horses, the clerk told him that Zeb at the livery had some fine pack horses,.

Big Jim told him he planned on picking up a few horses along the trail; the clerk gave him a funny look but said nothing. The clerk thinking to himself, where does that old trapper think he's going to get horses on the open prairie?

About five or six miles out of town, Big Jim looked for a buffalo hollow, he found a good one and dismounted and look over his back trail, sure enough the two men that were outside the assayers office were on his trail and up to no good.

Big Jim lay down at the top of the hollow and waited, with his flintlock and two pistols, he was not sure of the Hawkins cap and ball, he checked his primers then waited.

After a short wait the two men came riding up to the hollow, Jim stood up and with the flintlock cocked and ready.

"You boys don't take a warning very good do you"? Now the smart thing for you to do is drop those rifles.

One of the men spoke up, there are two of us old-timer and only one of you, do you think you can get us both?

"Well I will tell you greenhorn, I am going to count to three and the one still holding his rifle will die, one".

The two men looked at each other, Big Jim said two, and both men dropped their rifles.

"Now very carefully drop the pistols from your belts".

Both men did as he said.

"Now dismount".

When both were on the ground, Big Jim told them to strip off all their clothing.

The older of the two said: "Now hold on old timer".

Big Jim smiled and said "one".

They both got their clothes off as fast as they could.

"Fancy boots you two have, take them off too, Then Big Jim counted one".

Both men took off their boots real fast, and stood there in their long Johns.

Big Jim took an empty sack off his mule and told them to put all their clothes and boots in it and to put the sack on one of their horses.

I warned you boys back in town, but you did not take good advice, "Now start walking back to town, and you best walk fast it gets mighty cold on the prairie at night".

As the two men started walking, Big Jim said, "Oh thanks for the horses and guns, they will bring me a fine dollar or two".

One of the men said that's horse stealing.

Big Jim smiled, "Well you come looking for me in the mountains, and if you are unlucky to find me, I won't count, I will just shoot".

Big Jim picked up the guns, and put them on his new packhorses and distributed the goods from the mule to the horses. Big Jim scratched the mule's ears, it's nice to have some help Sara, don't ya think, and then he mounted his horse and headed off towards the mountains.

"I don't think we heard the last of them two, Sara".

Chapter 34

THE CONRAD BROTHERS CLEM AND ZEKE

The two Conrad brothers were as mad as anyone could be, they swore they would find that old man and kill him, and they wanted the money he had.

By the time they got back to town, it was dark and most of the stores were closed, they had no money to outfit themselves, so they decided to break into Preston's store.

The two looked all around to make sure no one was watching them, then they went down the alley to the back of the store, Zeke stepped on a board that had a nail in it and started hoping around and hollering, Clem slapped him on the back of his head.

"Shut up you dam fool".

"Well it hurts".

"Mom should have put you in that sack with the cats that she threw in the river, now stop your crying and help me get this door opened".

Together they forced the door open, once inside they found clothes and boots and got dressed, with Zeke still whimpering about his foot.

They took two rifles, powder, and ball and filled a sack with food, then went out the back door and headed for the stables. They found two saddles, took two horses out of the barn, and headed back the way they had come.

Zeke who was the crybaby, and said; they catch us they will hang us for horse stealing.

Stop your crying; when we kill the old man, we will turn the horses loose.

They mounted and headed back the way they had come, they pushed the horses hard knowing the old man was at least two days ahead of them.

Chapter 35

It was almost dark when Big Jim reached the pines at the base of the mountain; he knew he still had at least a three-day ride to the valley. He was in no hurry, and he knew the two men were following him, for he had seen their dust a long ways off, he would wait for them, no way was he letting them come to their valley.

Big Jim picketed the horses and Sara near the stream and the lush green grass, then built a small fire made his dinner and ate, then turned in for the night, he knew the two men would not reach him till mid morning.

Big Jim rose before the sun was up, there was coals still burning, so he added more wood making the fire much larger than he normally would, then made himself coffee, took his two rifles with him along with the pot of coffee, to higher ground.

Looking around, he saw a dead tree down on the ground, placing his two rifles across the log; he sat down and waited and drinking his coffee. When the sun was almost up, he looked across the plains and saw the two men about a mile away. He would give no warning this time, they planned on robbing and killing him, they were fools, and fools don't live long in the mountains.

As the two brothers were about a hundred yards from Big Jim's camp, they dismounted and tried to sneak up on the camp. Big Jim shook his head, and thought he had never seen two bigger fools in his life.

Big Jim took no pleasure in killing. But a man had to do what he had to do to survive in the mountains, he drew a bead on Clem, for he knew the other was a simpleton. Big Jim pulled back the hammer on his flintlock, at the sound of the click of the hammer being drawn back, Clem turned towards the noise. Big Jim pulled the trigger, there was a flash in the pan and then the big boom of the fifty-caliber gun, Clem's hands went up and he flew back, with a ball through his heart. Zeke just stood there like the simpleton he was, Big Jim picked up the new Hawkins cap and ball, pulled back the hammer and drew a bead on Zeke, but did not pull the trigger.

"Drop your rifle" Big Jim hollered.

Zeke did as he was told, Big Jim got up and walked down to where Zeke was standing and blubbering.

"Stop your blubbering, I'm not going to kill you, get your friend over his horse and get out of here, this is the last chance I will ever give you, and tell the clerk at the assayer's office that I will see him the next time I am in St Louis".

Zeke picked up his brother and put him over the back of his horse and rode away, still blubbering.

Big Jim picked up the two rifles and walked to where he had tied the horses, he put the packs on the two extra horses and saddled his, when he got to Sara he put the small pack and the two rifles on the pack.

"Well Sara, we got so many rifles we can open a trading post".

Big Jim Mounted and headed for home.

Climbing the mountain to the Valley was not easy for there were many switchbacks. Halfway up the mountain big Jim came face-to-face with Toomey, Toomey and big Jim reach for their rifles at the same time. Toomey, fired first his shot hit big Jim on the left side knocking him from his horse, the shot went through big Jim's side grazing Sara on the rump, Sarah took off squealing and bucking and ran up the mountain for home.

While laying on the ground big Jim drew his pistol and fired at Toomey, he did not know if he hit Toomey or not, but Toomey took off down the mountain like a shot.

Big Jim knew he was hit bad, for there was a lot of blood. Crawling over to the pack horse he got his water bag and what food he could get, then crawled over and got his rifle and dragged himself over to a large tree, Sitting with his back to the tree, he reloaded his pistol and waited to see if Toomey was coming back to finish him off.

Little did Big Jim know that his shot had hit Toomey in the chest and went through his left lung?

Chapter 36

Toomey was hit bad and he knew it, He thought if he had not went looking for that dam Crown he would not have been anywhere's near big Jim.

Toomey had waited for Crown to show up at the designated spot for a full day, the following morning he tracked Crown up the mountain, he could not imagine why Crown would go up the mountain, other than to find that Indian Girl. When he got to the top of the mountain he was surprised to find a beautiful valley, He looked all around and saw smoke off the far right of the valley, he headed for the smoke with great caution, when he got close enough he saw the cabin and the coral with Crowns horse in it.

Then he saw Skip feeding the horses, He then knew Crown must be dead, why else would Crowns horse be there. He turned his horse around and headed back down the mountain, he did not want to come across Big Jim.

Half way down the mountain is when he came face to face with Big Jim, he was more aware that he might come upon Big Jim than Big Jim was of meeting him that was the reason he got off the first shot.

He was coughing up huge amounts of blood; Toomey knew he was dying, for a shot in the lung was always fatal. He was about a mile away from where he shot Big Jim, when he fell off his horse. Even though it was early morning, it was growing very dark for Toomey.

His last thoughts were he should have lived a better life, for he knew he would soon meet his maker. But as all thief's and murderers, they think their time will never come. Then the gates of hell opened up for him also.

Chapter 37

After feeding the horses skip told Blue he was going to get some fresh meat, he saddled his horse and with dog following him he headed for the big pond, where he knew he would find a deer for they always came to the same spot for water.

About a hundred yards from the pond, Skip left horse, who was trained to stay where he was left, Skip went on foot to the pond, that was about half way between his cabin and Big Jims.

Upon reaching the spot where he always watched from, he sat down and watched the spot where the deer always drank, as he watched he noticed dogs ears turned up and was looking towards Big Jims Cabin, looking that way he could not see or hear anything, but dog kept looking that way and started whining.

"Dog what is it; no deer are going to come here if you keep that crying up". but dog would not stop.

"Alright dog go get horse and we will see what's bothering you".

Dog took off like a shot and with the reins in his mouth; Dog was soon back with horse.

Skip mounted horse, "Ok dog show me what's bothering you".

It did not take long for Skip to realize dog was headed for Big Jims place, so Skip nudged horse and took off at a gallop, upon reaching Jims cabin, he saw Sara trying to get in to the corral, The pack was still on Sara, but was hanging under her. Ship knew something was very wrong; he rode over to Sara dismounted and walked over to Sara who was very jumpy, talking very gentle he took the pack off Sara and let her into the corral, he saw the blood and the wound on her right flank. He now was very worried, He saw no other horses so he knew Big Jim was not there, He mounted horse, called dog, and headed down the mountain. Skip was worried that something terrible had happened to his friend and mentor. It was slow going down the mountain for all the switchbacks, skip kept his eye on dog knowing dog would warn him of any danger. about an hour after going down the mountain dog began to whine and get excited, skip knew that big Jim was close. He told dog to find big Jim, dog took off on a run and stopped near a tree and some brush.

Skip looked around and saw the three horses munching grass, he hollered out for big Jim but there was no answer. He rode horse over to the tree were dog was barking and saw big Jim leaning against a tree, he saw the blood on big Jim's side and got very scared, for Jim was not moving or talking. Skip dismounted from horse walk over to big Jim and called his name, big Jim opened his eyes and said" well boy took you long enough". Skip smiled and asked how bad was he hit. Big Jim said I'm hit in the side and I think I've got a broken rib but the ball went right through I think it hit the pouch with the Gold coins wrapped around my waist. Skip said let me have a look, we want to make sure that the gold is not hurt, they both gave a chuckle and skip took the pouch off from around big Jim's waist, skip examine the wound.

"I think we best see about getting you up this mountain and back to the cabin where Blue can look at this wound and treat it, we don't want it to get infected".

Skip packed all of belongings on the packhorses, help Jim get on his horse, and headed back up the mountain. Big Jim told skip to hold up, and told skip he wanted him to go down the mountain and see if he had hit Toomey. Skip and dog headed down the mountain, in a short time they come upon Toomey and his horse, he saw Toomey lying face down in the grass with blood all around, Skip knew that Toomey was dead, he dismounted and picked up Toomey's belongings and took his horse and headed back up the mountain.

When big Jim saw skip leading Toomey's horse, he knew he did not miss when he shot at Toomey, and had a big smile on his face for he had sworn to get even with Toomey for killing his friend. They continued up the mountain with skip leading the way, before too long they reached their Valley, skip told big Jim that he would have to stay at his cabin where blue could take care of him, big Jim smiled and said you will not get an argument from me, I kind of like her cooking. Skip gave a chuckle and said, guess you're not hurt too bad.

Chapter 38

With Blue taking care of Big Jim it was not long before he was well, The mountain air heals wounds much faster than down on the plains.

The fur trade was dying, so Skip and Big Jim kept searching for Gold in the stream, over time they had acquired a small fortune, more than they would ever need for they lived a quiet and peaceful life, their wants were not much, but they knew they had to plan, for their future.

Skip noticed that Big Jim was really slowing down, and this worried him, he did not know Big Jim's exact age but he knew he was close to ninety. Big Jim was a father to him, since that fateful day when he lost his parents.

At the end of the day, after panning for Gold, Skip told Big Jim, that they should take a few days off and just go hunting and fishing.

Big Jim was very tired, but did not want Skip to know about the pains he was getting in his chest and just how tired he was, and was all for a day of rest, and told Skip it sounded good.

The next morning while eating breakfast, Skip told Blue he was worried about Big Jim, and they were going to hunt and fish and just take it easy for a few days.

Dog started barking and carrying on, but skip could tell by the way dog was caring on that it was just his exciting bark. Skip picked up his rifle, even though he knew it was nothing to worry about, you just never went outside, unarmed, then went out the door, there was Dull Knife and his wife, Spotted Fawn sitting on their horses, with dog running around barking.

Skip smiled and asked them in for breakfast, Dull Knife said, they had already eaten but would like some coffee. They dismounted and followed Skip into the cabin. While sitting at the table drinking coffee, Skip told Dull Knife his plans, and how he was worried about Big Jim, and asked if he would like to come with them and that Spotted Fawn could stay and visit with Blue and the kids. Dull Knife excepted the invitation.

He hugged Blue and the kids, and they went out the door to the corral, Skip saddled Horse and they headed for Big Jims cabin, with old faithful Dog following him, Dog was not as spry as he used to be either, for he was getting on in years.

As they neared Big Jims cabin, Skip looked for smoke, but saw none and was worried, but as they came in sight of the cabin he could see Big Jim sitting on the porch with a cup of coffee and smoking his pipe, as they rode up to the porch,

Big Jim said: "You youngins sleep the day away, I been waiting since before the sun was up".

Skip smiled, "I see you have a pack on Sara".

"Yes I thought I would like to have her with me today, she is getting old".

Big Jim set his cup down knocked out his pipe and gingerly walked over to his horse and with great effort mounted.

'Well are we going to sit here all day"?

Skip and Dull Knife chuckled. Then turned their horses and headed for the big pond.

Very quietly, Skip said to Dull Knife, let's take it nice, and slow. Big Jim was no fool and knew what Skip was doing, but said nothing for his old bones were hurting.

They reached the big pond a little before noon, Skip said, "I am really hungry and could go for some nice fish, Big Jim why don't you see if you can catch us a passel of fish, while Dull Knife and I set up camp".

Big Jim smiled, "Sounds good to me".

Skip asked Dull Knife, "Why don't you see if you can get us a nice buck, I would like to stay close to Big Jim".

Dull Knife shook his head yes, "I understand my brother". Then Dull Knife took his bow, quiver, and walked off into the woods.

Skip unpacked the horses and Big Jims mule Sara, then set up camp, then with his pole in his hand walked down to the water near the big pine tree where Jim always sat when he fished and sat down next to Big Jim.

"Well are they biting"?

Big Jim pointed to his side where two big Trout were laying.

'A few more like that Big Jim and we will have enough for lunch".

They sat and talked about the old times, the hunting, fishing, and trapping they had done.

Skip looked over at his friend and father figure.

"Yes it was my lucky day when we stumbled upon you; I never would have made it in the mountains, without you and Dull Knife".

Big Jim smiled, "You come a long ways son".

Though Skip was close to forty, Big Jim always called him boy, this was the first time he called him son, and Skip liked it.

Soon they had all the fish they would need, and they decide to head for the camp.

Skip rose and gathered the fish, and noticed Big Jim was having a hard time getting up off the ground, he wanted to reach over and give him a hand, but knew Big Jim would not like that, so he just looked away, not wanting Big Jim to notice, he saw how hard it was for him to get up.

When they reached the camp, they saw Dull Knife coming out of the wood with a buck over his shoulder.

When Dull Knife reached the camp he slid the buck off his shoulder and looked at the passel of fish, "I guess we will eat good today".

They cleaned the Fish, skinned the Buck, and soon were eating trout and deer liver, they spent the day drinking coffee and talking over old times.

The sun was just going down when Big Jim said he was going to turn in, gingerly Big Jim got up, walked over to his robes, and was soon snoring.

They both gave a chuckle at Big Jims snoring.

They sat around talking, Skip said to Dull Knife; "Things are changing fast my brother, and the Indian must change with them, I know you want them to stay the way they are and so do I, but that won't happen. This is a big valley, we can build a cabin for you and Spotted Fawn, and your sister would like to have you here and so would I".

"I will think about it my brother, but now I am tired and will turn in, and hope I fall asleep before you start snoring, they both laughed and turned in for the night.

Skip laid in his robes, listing to the night sounds, the coyotes howling, the owl hooting, he was having a hard time falling asleep, for he was very worried about Big Jim, but soon sleep over took him.

Chapter 39

Just before dawn Skip and Dull Knife rose, started the fire, and put on the coffee, they decided to let Big Jim sleep till the coffee was done.

When the coffee was done, Skip walked over to Big Jim and gently shook him, "You going to sleep all day old man".

Big Jim did not move, so Skip shook him, but still he did not move, with tears in his eyes he knew his friend, mentor and adopted father was gone.

He turned to tell Dull Knife, but he saw Dull Knife was looking at him.

Dull Knife said: "I see the great sadness in your face my brother, we are born, we live, then we die, when the great Chief in the sky calls us we must go".

They buried Big Jim under the huge pine where Big Jim always sat when they fished at the pond.

They packed up their belongings, took Big Jims horse and Sara, who did not want to leave without her master.

Dog lay down on Big Jims grave and howled Skip called Dog to come, and they headed for skips cabin, along the way, Skip said: "I think Big Jim would be happy if you lived in his cabin".

"I will talk to Spotted Fawn about it".

The end.

Coming soon

By

Tony Monte.

Chapter 1

Eight Killers

The sun was hot and the eight men were worn and tired, their horses were almost done in, when the leader a big man with red hair, a red beard and a scar from his right eye down to his chin, saw smoke off in the distance, he reined his horse over to the right and the rest followed.

The last man in line, horse went down, the man tried to jump off but was not in time, he landed on his head with the horse on top of him, but no one stopped for him. He laid there in the dust not moving, for the fall had broken his neck. They were a tough bunch, and never looked back; it was every man for himself. Now there was Seven.

They rode into the yard and stopped in front of the small cabin. Big Red Carter looked around and saw the corral with eight horses in it. "Moffat watch the door, if anyone comes out, shoot them", then rode over to the corral, the rest followed.

John Pearson watched from inside the cabin, when he saw them roping his horses, he grabbed his shotgun and told his wife and son to stay inside, he opened the door, and stepped out onto the porch, "what do you think you're doing"? Without saying a word Moffat shot him in the gut, John Pearson fell off the porch face down in the dust.

Beth and Brodie Preston watched in horror as husband and father lay in the dust, Beth ran out screaming and Moffat shot her in the head, she was dead before she hit the ground, twelve-year-old Brodie ran out right behind her, and Moffat shot him. John Pearson did not have long to live, but had enough strength to reach the shotgun and blow Moffat out of the saddle, he looked over at his wife and son, and then died.

Now there were six.